RINGS OF BURNISHED BRASS

Modern Arabic Writing
from The American University in Cairo Press

Naguib Mahfouz	*Autumn Quail*
	The Beggar
	The Beginning and the End
	Midaq Alley
	Miramar
	Palace Walk
	(Volume I of *The Cairo Trilogy*)
	Respected Sir
	The Search
	The Thief and the Dogs
	Wedding Song
Mahmoud Manzalaoui (ed.)	*Arabic Short Stories 1945-1965*
William M. Hutchins (ed.)	*Egyptian Tales and Short Stories of the 1970s and 1980s*
Yusuf Idris	*The Cheapest Nights*
	Rings of Burnished Brass
Taha Hussein	*An Egyptian Childhood*

Rings of Burnished Brass

⬭⬭⬭⬭⬭⬭⬭

YUSUF IDRIS

Translated from the Arabic by
Catherine Cobham

The American University in Cairo Press

Dar el Kutub No. 7776/90
ISBN 977 424 248 3

Printed in Egypt by International Press

Contents

Introduction

⊙⊙⊙⊙⊙⊙

Yusuf Idris was born in 1927, in a small village near Ismailiyya in Egypt. After secondary school in the provincial capital he went to Cairo to study medicine in 1945, and published his first stories in *al-Miṣrī*, the Wafdist daily paper later banned by Nasser, in the late 1940s. He graduated in 1951 and practised medicine for several years, two of which were spent as government health inspector for Darb al-Ahmar, one of the most heavily populated areas of Cairo. Gradually writing claimed more and more of his concentration and attention and he had given up medicine for full-time writing and journalism by the middle 1960s.

His first collection of stories was published in 1954 and since then he has published several novels and plays and nine more collections of short stories. Four of his longer stories are translated below; *The Black Policeman* has recently been republished separately as a short novel.

The Stranger (1961) is the story of a young boy's relationship with an outlaw and murderer in the Egyptian countryside during the Second World War. The reader's attention is focused on the act of killing and the character of the killer as objects of fascination to the fourteen-year-old boy, but the action is inseparable from the village and the surrounding countryside which are portrayed through realistic details and in sharp unexpected moments of lyricism.

The boy first approaches the Stranger searching for manhood. In his mind the killing of a man represents the attainment of manhood and he looks to the Stranger and the 'Sons of the Night' to teach him their trade and provide him with the opportunity, outside the well-ordered confines of the village, to assume his virility. In the unfolding of the narrative his ideals of masculinity and virility, embodied in the Stranger, are severely challenged. As well as being exposed to the horror and fear involved in acts of killing, he himself, at the point where he is about to realize his ideal, experiences a startling, but improperly understood, revelation of the sacred inviolability of human life.

The Black Policeman (1962) is a sombre story of a torturer employed by the political police in the late 1940s, and one of his victims. Idris builds on facts: the case of 'the black policeman' was widely publicized in the Egyptian press in the 1950s, and he uses this recent history to comment on events contemporary to the time of writing.

The narrator and Shawqi, the torturer's one-time victim, are intellectuals of Idris' own generation who had been politically active in rival groups before 1952. In seeking to understand the disturbing changes in his rival, now his colleague, the narrator, aided by various subsidiary characters, traces the effect of torture, and the lasting fear and mental and spiritual disfigurement caused by it in the victim and in the torturer. The behaviour of the latter is partly illuminated by accounts of the way he was treated in his native village in Upper Egypt, and at the hands of his employers, particularly a senior government minister who, regarding him lewdly as a perfect physical specimen, shows him off to his guests in his *salon*.

There is much reference to dehumanization and bestiality in the narrative and the whole is a documentation of fear and 'man's inhumanity to man'. It is perhaps irrelevant that many torturers may pass through life without suffering too much as a result of their *métier*. The effort of compassion, or the concentration of pity, made by the author, does not produce a sentimental melodrama referring to an isolated case, but charts a distorting of human values through complete isolation to spiritual death, in the torturer and his victim respectively.

The Siren (1969) is the drama of a surrender, that of the peasant woman Fathiyya to the Man in the Suit, which continually interrelates with and comments upon her surrender to urban civilization, to Cairo, the sea from which 'thousands of hands stretched out' to her, deceptively alluring. To Fathiyya, the sexual relationship that the Man intimates to her, terrifying her and making her retreat within herself, represents the most wicked aspect of the capital, 'like a dreadful hand stretching out, threatening to pull her down into the mud and filth' at the bottom, but at the same time it fascinates her. Moreover she rationalizes the disagreeable aspects of the city to herself and is aware of the need to guard against disillusion, to protect herself from actually *seeing* the 'slime at the bottom', which so shocked Emma Bovary after her own surrender.*

The image of her aggressor, the Man in the Suit, as a wolf or hyena, with all its echoes in folklore and common usage, runs through the narrative. He is a flatter character than Fathiyya or her husband, Hamid, a caricature in whom potential virtues and attractive features have degenerated into weapons for exploiting extreme weakness in others as a means to self-gratification.

Sex and related standards of physical beauty and ideals of masculinity and femininity are portrayed in a way which illuminates the cultural differences between the country and the city, and particularly the 'cultural shock' experienced by peasants emigrating from the countryside, when they are faced by the fluctuating undefined values of the city. The torment and confusion of Hamid in the moments following the discovery of his wife's infidelity are described minutely. The startling opening paragraphs arrest the reader's attention and bridge the gap of experience between him and the emigrant peasant, the porter living in a room under the stairs in a large block of flats. At the same time the quality of slow motion which is imparted to his movements by the way they are described makes him removed, and isolated for scrutiny, like a figure in a dance or mime.

The notion of surrender or submission is central to Idris' dramatization of Egyptian characteristics on both an individual and a national scale, and is fertile ground for confronting the self-deceptions connected with a deterministic or fatalistic outlook, and the actual part played by the individual will. Fathiyya's own view of her predicament is persistently fatalistic and yet within the framework of such an outlook she herself has doubts, and the whole action is portrayed with an irony that leaves the reader with little doubt that the events were not simply determined by fate, and that the fatal elements had a precisely defined nature.

The irony culminates at the point where, during the scene of the 'rape' of Fathiyya and her 'surrender', something happens

---

* Flaubert, *Madame Bovary*, trans. Alan Russell, Penguin, 1950, p. 183.

which the fateful voices had never mentioned and 'the submission imposed on her by defeat' begins to change momentarily into 'submission born of enjoyment' before Hamid enters. Here the irony is no more or less at Fathiyya's expense than it has been at any point in the narrative, and there is no suggestion that the use of force, at either the literal or metaphorical level of meaning in the plot, is condoned for a moment. How adequately the contradictions, and unknown or unknowable elements of the conflict, are taken into account is demonstrated by the effect of the ending, which appears as both surprising and inevitable.

Rings of Burnished Brass (1969) tells of an encounter between a well-off middle-aged woman and a poor boy of eighteen. The woman's children no longer respond to her maternal love and the boy is motherless, and the feelings of mother and woman and son and lover are woven intricately together in the narrative. The emphasis of the story, unlike the previous one, is partly on sexuality itself, or rather on the importance of, and the nature of, erotic attraction, and its relationship to other attachments and affections, whether spiritual, emotional, or enforced by convention.

Like a pioneering attempt in the visual arts to depict the naked human body from this perspective without being either coy or pornographic, the story has some exaggerated lines and awkwardnesses. Most of the action is viewed from within the mind of the lonely middle-aged woman, and any clumsiness derives from the author's earnestness to show rapidly changing emotions, or the simultaneous existence of conflicting but equally sincere emotions; and, more importantly, to press his claim that human sexuality goes beyond physical sensation to some ultimate mystery.

He takes a situation which would appear from the outside as a trivial one, possibly sordid, or merely pitiful and ridiculous, and shows the tortuous thoughts and feelings which surround it, and also the grace of the two central characters' actions, the importance of each feeling, and the reality of their passion.

Unlike Fathiyya in *The Siren*, the woman in the story is conscious of her own exploitation of the idea of the intervention of fate or destiny, and of her moral obligation to exert her will, or use her mind, which Idris calls without embarrassment 'a strange and magical member' of the human body. But because of the confusing nature of her feelings, and of the reality surrounding her, she does no more than temporarily and imperfectly assert her independence from customs and habits and family obligations, before bleakly accepting the fate imposed on her by these very conventions and her own weakness.

The author's attempt to discover ways of expressing intangible areas of experience is given shape and perspective because the story's action is embedded so firmly in a particular time and place. Nothing illustrates this better than the glimpses of the women's family, particularly the vignette of their Friday visits to her. These representatives of the new Nasserite and post-Nasserite Egypt are shown as reasonable, secular and conventional with their unprecedented level of education and resulting positions of power and wealth; they are also hypocritical, materialistic and without love, but in these areas of which he is a master Idris never overstates.

The subtitle, 'A story in four squares', refers to the four sections into which it is divided, and perhaps to the four equally important elements of the relationship between the woman and the boy; it also draws attention to the relevant physical features of the places which recur in the story, the large square tiles of the floor by the door in the mosque where the woman loses her balance and is saved by the boy, and the square tiles on the floor of the room whose worn edges pierce into her back as she lies with him.

In my translation of these stories I cannot hope to have faithfully represented the originals, for 'faithful representation' is a far from unambiguous concept. This is not to say that I have interpreted rather than translated: in fact I found that I moved closer to literalness in the course of translating them, or found surprisingly that there was more scope for licence in choice of words, but less in syntax, than I had anticipated. A commentator on Ezra Pound's translations, Hugh Kenner, has written '. . . as the poet begins by seeing, so the translator by reading; but his reading must be a kind of seeing'.* I hope that in these translations I have 'seen' at least something of what Idris intends, and perhaps shown that 'Languages are not strangers to one another, but are, a priori and apart from all historical relationships, interrelated in what they want to express.'**

The Translations of Ezra Pound, introduced by Hugh Kenner, Faber, 1953, p. 10.
**W. Benjamin, *Illuminations*, Fontana, 1973, p. 72.

The Stranger

⦿⦿⦿⦿⦿⦿

No one would have guessed that Shurbagi, fair-haired and rosy-cheeked, with vivid attractive features, had hidden in his past an unlikely history of encounters with a hardened killer, a brigand – a Lord of the Night. My time-honoured friend from secondary school days, he had shown me how to ride a bicycle and write stories, and had fostered my addiction for paperback novels; and I myself would have found it hard to believe, before he told me the story, that there was an episode in his life of which I knew nothing at all.

We only ever came together by chance although we both worked in the same city. Each time we would exchange addresses and arrange to meet, knowing instinctively that we wouldn't keep to the arrangements, that it would take another chance meeting to bring us together again. I had once met his father, and I knew which village his family came from, trivial details like his passion for women, his intense irritation that, even though we had grown up and left school we still called him by his surname as we always had done. His real name was Abd al-Rahman Salih al-Shurbagi, but at school we had tired of all the common, much-used first names and had known him as Shurbagi, and the name had stuck, so much so that I was taken by surprise when his wife called him Abd al-Rahman in front of us.

Still I had no idea that he, a man of exemplary manners, whose sensitivities were offended by so much as a word out of place, even when he was a grown man with children of his own, had ever been involved with people like the Stranger, and the blood-letting of the outlawed underworld. Chance, as I say, was responsible for my knowing, helped perhaps by the fact that it was the middle of the night and we were talking about killing and killers. Shurbagi

---

Al-Gharib ('the stranger') is the character's given name in Arabic, which in this particular case it seemed preferable to translate into English throughout.

was neither an eloquent speaker, nor a very good story-teller, although he was the one who had taught me how to write stories, but he spoke with more artistic sense than he wrote. I don't know what led him to disclose this part of himself on that particular occasion: perhaps, as I have said, it was something to do with the hour and the tale itself but more likely it had to do with the obvious delight with which he plunged inside himself, digging deep and emerging with treasures whose very existence he seemed to be aware of for the first time. This pleasure, so clear to me as I watched him, drove him on; he talked all night and I listened, and shuddered from time to time, but my attention never wandered.

1

Can you imagine that there were times in my life when all I could think about was killing somebody, for no other reason than the desire to kill for its own sake? Don't go searching in your medical textbooks or looking up recent developments in psychology to try and find a scientific explanation for these whims of mine. I wasn't sick or abnormal, and I hadn't suffered as a result of any tragedies in the family. I was a perfectly ordinary schoolboy, not much more than fourteen, and I always assumed that mine was a natural desire and one that was not peculiar to me. Surely from time to time most of us assert ourselves in some unprecedented way to prove to ourselves that we are men, and boys on the brink of manhood are especially prone to this? They leave home to look for work, stay out all night, begin to play around with their fathers' guns and, if the fathers object, threaten to shoot themselves or anyone standing in their way – the implication being obvious. They confirm their manhood to themselves in the rough crude ways of men.

The only difference between me and my peers was that I over-reached a little in my desire, and wanted to enter the world of men by killing one of them. In general I kept this buried deep, not daring to disclose it even to myself, although I was aware of its existence and made attempts to realize it as it were behind my own back; this was because I was afraid that I wouldn't stop at killing one man, that once I had started out in this way I would be compelled to go on, but I reassured myself continually, saying that it would never happen.

As proof of this I expounded to myself my past experience with cats. When I was a small child I had been very frightened of them – their long moustaches, snarling faces and ugly-looking claws – and looked longingly forward to the day when I would grow big enough to frighten them in turn, exacting my revenge for all the misery they had caused me. Growing older was connected in my mind with an increasing ability to terrorize cats and hence with freeing myself from my fear of them. With this end in view I pursued them constantly, trying to drive them into corners and enjoying the sight of their suffering at my hands. However many cats I chased, however many doors and windows I closed to block off their escape routes, I never managed to barricade one in successfully, except once, when I shut the neighbours' cat up in a room in our house. We disliked our neighbours and I decided not to stop at frightening the cat and enjoying the spectacle of her fear, but to go further and put her to death.

I chased her relentlessly until I had her in the storeroom where all the apertures were firmly secured, and I went in behind her armed with an iron rod, one of the uprights from an old window, and shut the door. I took the greatest conceivable delight in the cat's predicament as she leapt from the ground to the roof and back again, searching, terrified, for a way out, uttering cries of alarm all the while. Everything about her seemed to stand on end and tremble as I approached her with measured step, the iron bar raised high above my head ready to deliver the single deadly blow.

I drew near to her gradually, relishing the state of paralyzing fear which had taken hold of her, exacting recompense for all the fear that I had suffered when I was little, happy with myself, my new-found stature, and this magnificent opportunity for revenge. Then suddenly I stopped short; after her violent frantic attempts to escape the cat had realized, or so it seemed to me, that there was no way out – I can still remember her last despairing cry from the gloomy corner where I had driven her. Then she turned round to face me for the first time since I had started chasing her and clawed at the ground and began advancing towards me. It was

then that I looked at her and noticed her eyes; I'll never forget the
all-consuming, quintessential fear that I saw there. With her
pupils completely dilated, teeth bared to their utmost, consummate fear written all over her, she had reached the point, I am
sure, when she was ready to spring and attach herself to me; she
would go for my throat, embedding her teeth and nails into my
flesh, tearing at my face and gouging out my eyes. One look was
enough – for a moment I was rooted to the spot, immobile in the
face of her mad desperate fear, then, just in time, I found enough
strength to run out of the room, not looking to right or left. I
searched for my mother, to fling myself trembling into her arms
and bury my face, my eyes, in her breast, wishing in vain to be
wholly submerged in her.

The excessive behaviour which led me to affirm that I had left my
childhood behind me and acquired some physical strength by
terrorizing cats, when once upon a time I had been so frightened
of them myself, perhaps developed naturally into my later
excesses. I abandoned my escapades with cats once and for all
after what happened to me in the storeroom, and had I known the
much more dreadful situation that I was to get into as a result of
wanting to show the world that I was a man, I might have
hesitated a little. As it was, I gave free rein to my desires, and in
my heart of hearts had made up my mind, albeit secretly, to
pursue them relentlessly to the end.

I'm sure you'll say that my conceiving of killing as a means to
this end was a continuation of the tendencies I had shown when I
was little, but in fact this was not the case. It was not the act for
its own sake, but those who did it who fascinated me. Where I
come from they are known as the 'Sons of the Night', those who
hold sway in the night-time and kill anybody who gets in their
way. At that age they held a great attraction for me: I dreamed of
joining the ranks of those who made ordinary mortals, happy
with their miserable lot, tremble at the mention of their name.
For me, the Sons of the Night embodied the ideals of manhood, a
concept linked in my mind with extraordinary acts performed by
extraordinary men, and I wanted to be identified with them
because it was the men of our village whose mundane calm they
disturbed.

In short, I wanted to become a hero, since that's what being a real man meant to me, and so I was continually following the movements of my idols, my own heroes, down to the most trivial detail, with the same passionate ardour that the youth of today reserve for the doings of film stars and rock singers. I dreamt of getting to know them, or any one of them, and in my dreams we would make friends and he would teach me his trade, show me how to kill, and I would come out of the experience a man.

As I said, I was just about fourteen, skinny, pale, docile-looking. I had never quarrelled, certainly never come to blows with anyone in my whole life, and my mother and father and everyone that knew me used to say that I was a good-natured, well-behaved child. They never knew that inside me I felt as if I was about to erupt and that in my head I carried dreams of a strange secret world quite different from the pale stagnating one that I lived in from day to day. In my world there was courage and valour, the stakes were high and the danger of conflict ever present; it was a world of darkness, and only a hero, a Child of the Night, could enter it and survive.

2

I tried all the ways that were open to me to get closer to them. I was bored with the company of my contemporaries at the village school and roamed about the cafés and places where the men gathered listening out for news of a theft or of any sort of crime, and hoping that I'd come across someone who'd seen something and was ready to talk. My saviour always turned out to be Mr. Khalil, watchman over the tomato crop on a nearby estate. By then he was quite an old man, but in his youth he'd been a criminal and an outlaw of some notoriety – perhaps his employers had taken this into account and considered it a good qualification for guarding two hundred acres of tomatoes.

I used to take him tobacco, sugar and tea, especially tea for he was addicted to it; he would put all of it into the boiling water at once and then make three different brews, the first with no sugar at all, the second with just a touch, and the third sweet, and only then was I allowed to drink some. Sitting with Mr. Khalil was for

me the ultimate enjoyment, and when the tea and the tobacco
had done their work, elevating his senses and lending him an air
of authority, he began to talk of his adventures: of the famous
criminals he had known – the cattle they had rustled, the walls
they had tunnelled their way through, the houses they had
broken into. I liked the way he never made himself out to be much
of a hero, and didn't exaggerate the importance of the parts he
played: whomever he was working with, he always seemed to
have acted as look-out, bringing up the rear and giving warning of
any danger.

I think he found pleasure in my company too; he was old and
alone, and he squatted day and night in the hut he had made for
himself at the top end of the tomato plantation. He only had one
eye and he tied a grubby scarf of local design over the place where
the other should have been, in such a way that it didn't appear to
be hiding a disfigurement. He loved to talk and in me he had
found his best audience. He talked for hours, never tiring, while
my untutored imagination caught fire, and I was consumed with
a passion not only to listen, but to do something, join a gang, for
example, and see them in action. So I used to ask him if he knew
any of the modern counterparts, whose exploits we heard
snippets of news about here and there, and he would answer
scornfully, gesturing in a despairing sort of way: 'They're kids.
You're talking about the old days . . . but now . . . they don't
really know what they're doing.'

I had to believe him, since, judging from the stories I had
heard, it was obvious that the men and the times he talked of
belonged to a glorious world that had gone for ever. I continually
regretted not having been born a few years earlier, resentful that a
time so full and splendid should have eluded me. There was only
one person whose name Mr. Khalil didn't respond to with a
dismissive wave of the hand when I questioned him. Instead he
would look dejected and say, 'Ah . . . the Stranger. Abu
Muhammad. He's a real man. The only one left over from the old
days'. That was because the Stranger was already known far and
wide as the man who had the police running around in circles;
since he wasn't of the generation that Khalil knew about, I
realized, even at the age I was then, that while he couldn't deny
the Stranger his place in folklore, he accounted for his daring and

courage, the way he had assumed the proportions of a hero, by claiming that he was a throwback to the old days.

I used to ask him repeatedly if he could introduce me to the Stranger, let me see him just once, and he would try to wriggle out of it, making it clear that he felt he'd been too open with me: 'You don't want to have anything to do with people like that, son. They're evil and you'd do best to keep clear of them.'

His response didn't upset me at all: of course he wouldn't want to admit to himself that he was the same person who moments before had sung the praises of the Sons of the Night, and glorified their way of life and treated their leaders as heroes. And when it came to himself having been one of them he would repeat in a voice of mortal fear that God had looked kindly on him, it had all been a long time ago and now he had repented and said his prayers, and, thank God, fasted in Ramadan. None of this was true, and I'd seen with my own eyes men going to him to hide things in his hut, and coming back after a few days to retrieve them. I'd seen them slipping money to him furtively, and I'd been with him when he was called away and then came back, obviously disturbed, and said to me in a distracted tone of voice, 'Ah, yes now . . . what was it we were talking about?'

Then he'd launch into a story that I'd heard before and I'd put up with it for a bit hoping that it might turn out to be different; then when every detail was the same, I'd tell him, and he'd go on to another adventure, and again I would have heard it before. Yet when I'd discovered that he had no more new stories to tell, I didn't stop visiting his hut. (He called it 'the aeroplane' and kept watch from it with his one weak clouded eye over the vast acreage of tomatoes.) I didn't stop because deep down I considered him a means of access to the Stranger, the only link I knew of, for I still hoped to come across him one day although the summer holidays were fast dwindling, the days rushed past, and while my curiosity and eagerness to see him increased, my hopes were nearly running out.

I never really imagined that before the end of the holidays I would have got to know the Stranger, and still less did I picture how I would meet him.

3

The Second World War was at its height and Rommel was in El Alamein. People were talking about Haj Muhammad Hitler and the proclamation of his conversion to Islam, and they expected him to arrive one day and throw out the British for us. But the underworld in our district was preoccupied with matters that had no connection with Hitler or Rommel: a military edict had gone out ordering the transferring of all suspected criminals to a prison in the Sinai Desert; people with scores to settle were busy conducting smear campaigns and every district commissioner and every village major had his work cut out, aided and abetted by the malicious and the resentful. Every few days a detachment of people was despatched to Sinai, handcuffed and in chains, some of them real criminals, other just profiteers or innocent people wrongfully accused.

Our district was blessed with a commissioner who was related to one of the King's men – whom there's been so much talk about in the press – and so he thought he could interpret the military edict in his own way. Instead of giving himself the trouble of organizing the operation, with all the paper-work that was involved, he arranged for the suspects to be transported, not to Sinai but to the next world. This he managed in an exquisitely simple way which did not even call for chains or handcuffs; if he succeeded in getting his hands on one of them, instead of putting him in prison, he kept him in his room and made conversation with him, offered him cups of tea and cigarettes and generally put him at his ease. Then when night fell he would invite him to go for a drive with him in the Ford truck, and there, on the edge of the lake, or beside one of the gloomy canals leading to it, he would stop the truck and get out, invite his guest to do the same, then with a few shots dispose of him and throw him into the lake. And whether or not his body was washed up at some stage was immaterial, since nobody had seen anything and nobody knew what was going on, least of all the government who in their edict had not been insistent that the criminal or suspect should necessarily remain alive. It would, after all, be beyond the powers of any official enquiry to establish precisely the limit of their responsibility towards the man in police custody, or anyone else for that matter.

The incidence of these infamous excursions – if I can call them that – rose alarmingly, and they became public knowledge. They enabled the zealous commissioner to get rid of any number of criminals, indeed anybody with a record, until his murderous exploits were more talked about than the doings of even the most venerated bandit. He got to hear what people were saying about him and laughed, so heartily that it could be heard ringing out noisily from the windows of his office in the district headquarters. Perhaps he too found that the pleasure to be derived from stepping outside the confines of the law far surpassed the pleasure of applying it.

In his private conversations, or when he addressed his subordinates, he was apparently fond of repeating that none of what had happened till then was of much significance, and that he would not rest until he had been for a drive with the Stranger, Abu Muhammad, acknowledged leader of the underworld in our district, if not in the whole of Lower Egypt. He was not at all satisfied with the efforts of the local security services, and every day he had a row of them up in front of him to reprimand them for their inefficiency. It was said that on these occasions he used expressions that a down-and-out wouldn't dream of using. Strange for somebody that was reputed to owe his influence to his palace connections.

In spite of all the measures he took the Stranger remained at large somewhere in the countryside, and the thing clearly assumed the dimension of a personal challenge, rather than remaining even theoretically a matter of law enforcement. The commissioner began to spend his own money on the operation – or perhaps it wasn't exactly his own money; rewards were ready in anticipation of a coup and he hired spies and made a play for Shalabi, known to be the Stranger's right-hand man. This last move seems to have been the one that paid off, for one day the local people learnt to their surprise that the Stranger was locked up awaiting his fate as a result of some arrangement that the authorities had come to with Shalabi, who had himself been arrested earlier.

There was a further surprise when at sunset they announced

that the Stranger had escaped in the heat of the day. They were after him, and anyone found hiding him or deliberately concealing his whereabouts would meet with the direst fate imaginable.

The local people couldn't get over this news. They talked about it for days afterwards, and became like people watching a game of cops and robbers from the sidelines. But it was a dangerous game and they looked on surreptitiously, and discussed it in secret, in subdued voices. Neighbour reproved neighbour and friend cautioned friend, reminding each other of the commissioner's spies watching their every move, sniffing out the Stranger's whereabouts.

A group of us, schoolboys and students, were sitting on the stone wall of the bridge one night, discussing the big hunt; we were quite confident that there was no spy or secret policeman in our midst, yet still we were fearful and spoke in whispers. And when we became absorbed in our conversation to the exclusion of all else, one of us warned, 'The night has ears. We'd better shut up,' and we were shaken out of our carelessness, and fell silent.

In our silence the fear began to be oppressive. Everybody knew that the Stranger hadn't left the area, and was stepping up his challenge to the commissioner, taking advantage of the high summer corn, whose tall stalks interlacing would have hidden a runaway elephant. When we talked we felt danger threatening us from two sides: from the commissioner and his informers, and from the Stranger himself. For who could guarantee that we might not let slip a word of praise for either one of them and incur the wrath of the commissioner and his men, or anger the Stranger, who, they said, wore a knife strapped to the calf of his leg.

To be sitting there talking at all was a kind of recklessness which would certainly result in harsh words, even beatings: our parents, like everyone round about, had been in a state of chronic terror from the moment they knew that the Stranger had escaped and was hiding in the fields, and came out at night sometimes to get food and cash. But their fear too was double-edged, and so much did they not want to be accused of protecting the Stranger, even unwittingly, that they dispensed with the evening prayer and the cattle came home before sunset. The fields and streets turned into a bleak wasteland at night-time, where nothing stirred except grim armoured patrols touring the shadows of the deserted night in search of the wolf lurking there.

Because all these thoughts passed rapidly through our minds when we stopped talking, we didn't stop for long. Almost immediately somebody said something and the others were quick to join in, and the conversation, in spite of our efforts, resumed its original course. The question we asked each other, which really meant that each of us was asking himself, was: 'What would you do if you met the Stranger on your way home?' A cold blast of fear swept over us at the very idea: although secretly we might have almost wished it would happen, these little whisperings were quickly suppressed by a million louder voices within us. Then the defence mechanisms of cowardice sprang into action taking upon themselves all the trappings of courage, and making courage look like rashness, even madness, or stupidity.

The fear became too much, and whereas before it had kept us where we were, unable to move, now it broke up the gathering; some sought safety in numbers and clung together, one begging another to go with him to the door of his house, and others simply decided to go by the route where there were most houses. But, as for me, when I stood up to leave, could it be that I had some faint premonition of what was going to happen that made me feel almost light-hearted?

4

I couldn't say categorically that I had no such premonition, but it wasn't anything like a sixth sense or a revelation from the unknown – more an overwhelming feeling of detachment that came over me making me think that things would be much the same whether I met him or not.

To get to our house I had to go along the canal bank with my companions and then, while they went on their way to the village, I left them and turned up a narrow track that led round the edge of the village, with dwellings on one side of it and cultivated land on the other. The curious thing was that I only felt frightened when I was with the others, and when I was left on my own this fear suddenly evaporated. But still a great unease swept over me as if the fear had reached such a pitch that I no longer responded to it consciously and yet was on the alert, ready to defend myself in an almost demented fashion, sensitive to every slightest sound, my febrile imagination translating every whiteness in the night into a gallabiyya, every blackness into a shadow, every flicker of movement into a knife thrust.

I had only a few yards to go alongside the field of corn before I reached the lower-growing wheat which offered fewer possibilities for concealment and was therefore more reassuring for me. At night the rough-edged, razor-sharp leaves of the corn plants whisper together and catch you unawares in the face, or cut your hands, but I couldn't slow down for fear that every second might bring disaster. Then I heard a sound at my back. At first I thought it was a dog barking. But it was a voice: 'Lad!'

An order from another human being. I took a step forward and this time it came clearly, silencing the whispering leaves and the crickets' strident drone.

'Lad!'

It penetrated my senses, staccato and imperious. Then I felt a burning deafness as if hot water had been poured into my ears and I could no longer hear, or move, or breathe, but a single thought pounded through my mind: 'It's happened. It's happened. It's happened.'

It took only a moment, but it consumed hours' worth of moments afterwards, of sitting down and reconstructing the events, making them submit to logic and reason. For I didn't run when I could so easily have done; I stopped my dry throat from crying out, even my breath from coming. And I swung round with a sudden scared movement, and when I spoke the shrill hoarseness in my adolescent voice gave me something of a grown man's hard tones:

'Yes. What do you want?'

'Don't be afraid, sonny.'

Was that a reasonable proposition? Could it be that fear is sometimes responsive to an order – if it comes from a particular person – to such an extent that you may actually find that you have stopped yourself being afraid as a result? If not, how was I able on that occasion to push away my fear? My body was seized by a trembling, but with none of the usual accompanying sensations, as if the fear had abandoned my head, and my heart, to reside only in my limbs.

My chief concern then became to summon my will-power and bring it to bear on this involuntary expression of fear. To no avail. On the contrary the more I tried, the more violent the shaking became. The one thing I knew was that I must not show that I was afraid, and a question burst from me, almost unexpected: the only thought behind it was to stop my teeth chattering, my knees quaking – to get through the next few moments at any price. Somehow I thought that if this could be done then I would be able to gather my wits about me and conduct myself appropriately.

'Who's that?'

I bellowed it, in a voice worthy of the commissioner himself or even the Stranger, if one could imagine him being approached by some unsolicited person along his way. And quickly before my teeth had time to begin chattering again, I repeated:

'Who are you?'

The voice answered – and up till then I was uncertain whether it came from behind me or in front of me or from the very bowels of the earth:

'I'm a stranger.'

Like a frightened man firing blindly till his ammunition runs out, I burst into speech once more. I was about to say 'a stranger or the Stranger?', but instinctively I caught the question in flight and made myself say:

'You're the ... Why were you shouting lad at me like that? Aren't you going to say good evening, my friend? Why don't you say good evening?'

My ammunition ran out then, and I fell silent, and the other voice did not reply. I was no longer deaf; the hum of night came back to me and my breathing grew regular and deeper. I began to think about taking to my heels, shouting for help as I went, but I knew inside me that I would do nothing of the sort, that I couldn't have moved an inch even if I had wanted to.

To me the silence seemed to go on for a long time. I thought everything must be over and the owner of the voice gone away, but then I became convinced that I was being studied by two hidden eyes and that my state of mind and my extreme youth must be discovered immediately. This was going to be my moment of truth and how the sensation disturbed me as I stood there bareheaded and barefoot, under a sky whose cold moon was slowly fading away, choked by the covering darkness. I stood frozen to the spot as the unseen eyes, directed at me from somewhere in the dense undergrowth, scrutinized me at their leisure. It was not terror that immobilized me, but the aftermath of terror, the same thing that keeps a mouse in a trap dead still so that even if the trap opens, he stays where he is.

From the darkness softened by the branches' shadows I heard a laugh, not the kind of laugh that it was possible to evaluate, for, compared to the real thing, it was a single bead of a rosary, a tiny drop of water, a shred of material handed over by a salesman as a specimen. Much to my surprise, it angered me. More than that, I felt myself actually suppressing my rage, but I kept silent.

'Who's your father, sunshine?'

The question stung me into action, especially the word 'sunshine'; and yet I felt curiously at ease. When I answered he started to speak: 'Your father's a good man . . .' but I didn't hear the rest: the branches swayed and rustled and from amongst them appeared a slightly built woman dressed in black with a headshawl and a veil whose gold brocade glimmered faintly in the light of the yellow moon.

5

Some people might think that in these clothes he became an object of scorn and derision, but the exact opposite was true. I felt my hair stand on end and my scalp tingle when I saw the Stranger – notorious killer, scourge of the province – wearing a black dress and veiling himself like a woman. Evil in conventional forms is frightening but when it comes diminutively, like a weasel from the undergrowth, it is sinister and dreadful, more terrifying by far.

He took a few steps in my direction and the voice inside my head kept telling me to run but then he sat down suddenly and invited me to do the same. This I did although I affected a certain deliberation and exaggerated slowness. The edge of the irrigation ditch didn't look like a comfortable place to sit but I was more concerned about the Stranger's motives – as far as I knew he only had dealings with people when he wanted their money, or was going to kill them, so I wondered what he wanted with me since he hadn't killed me and couldn't possibly think that I had any money on me.

I sat there without saying anything. I'd intended to talk but was kept in check by that instinctive wariness which asserts itself when we don't know the intentions of those we are with, especially when they are potentially dangerous. Even at this stage I didn't really feel that I had seen him properly, although I was acutely aware of him there beside me, and tried to examine him. He seemed impregnable, shielded by the network of stories and folklore that had grown up around him over a long period, woven from tales of his murder victims, accounts of him as hunter and hunted, and conflicting pictures of the bold outlaw and the wanted criminal. In spite of it or because of it, I couldn't seem to see him. The woman's clothes made the problem worse, adding a genuine barrier to the one in my head, so that I felt he was both there and not there, and an air of fantasy hung about his person and his speech.

I imagined to myself that the black figure beside me was only the shadow of the giant of my fancy who still lurked hidden in the corn, or that the clothes were empty and that the Stranger was nothing more than a fragment of quicksilver inside them, impossible to catch hold of and pin down.

He took a packet of cigarettes from his pocket – or that's what I hoped he was doing, for every time he moved I jumped, expecting the knife that he was said to keep strapped around his leg to be plunged into my chest.

'Have a cigarette?'

'No thank you very much.'

In those days I used to smoke secretly, one or two a day, and I said, feigning politeness, 'I don't smoke.'

Mocking me he shook his head: 'Oh yes, you do . . . come on, take one.'

I pretended that he had been too clever for me: 'If it will make you happy, I'll take one.'

He handed me a cigarette and then struck a match and

extended it to me.

I swore to myself that I wouldn't be the first to light up but his only response was to blow out the match. Then he brought his face close to mine, the veil raised a little so that he could light his cigarette, and struck another match. Both of us came closer to it to stop it going out. The match blazed, lighting up the space between us, and there – God forbid – was his face, the face of a she-devil with eyes strangely elongated or a mad satanic ewe wearing a veil.

The cigarette fell out of my mouth – the only way I knew that my mouth was open. This time I was really frightened, and it was as if all the fear that I had felt before had been only the fits of yawning which precede an illness, and that when I stared at his face, that was the cold enervating fever of fear, the illness itself.

But then what strange abilities we humans beings demonstrate in certain situations. Had I acted instinctively, I would have lost my head out of sheer terror and turned and run until I dropped, or he caught up with me. As it was I sat down beside him, actually empowered by the acuteness of my fear to control myself. I smoked the strong local cigarette he had offered me, and my head went round, for I wasn't very used to smoking, and certainly not to inhaling.

I answered his questions with conviction, or at least with sincere desperate attempts to sound convincing, and most of the time I succeeded, and my answers came out clear, reasonable, almost natural. He asked me where our house was in relation to where we were sitting, where I had been, whom I had been with, what I'd said to them and what they'd said to me, and what people said about him. Even in the strange state that I was in, I couldn't have failed to notice how childishly happy it made him to hear the things I told him, however trifling some of them were, about his image in the eyes of other people. Some of them I invented, which came very easily to me, anxious as I was to please him: I contrived to show him to himself in a magnifying mirror which doubled his size and blew up his heroic exploits till they appeared as imposing as a minaret or a date palm in the flat countryside that surrounded us.

As I took the last few drags of my cigarette I was still painfully aware that I wanted to tell him how often I had tried to meet him, and call Mr. Khalil – whose 'aeroplane' was not far off – as my witness. I hesitated because I was afraid that I would explain myself in a way that would incur his anger, and the thing I was most eager to avoid just then was saying anything or making any move that would annoy him. It seemed to me that he might even flare up suddenly for no reason, like a madman – as if I imagined the ethics of outlaws and the insane to be very similar. But then all such speculations went out of my mind and I became oblivious to everything except the pincers which attached themselves to my earlobe as I bent to bury my cigarette stub in the earth.

Fingers. If they were fingers they must have had joints of iron covered with skin that had dried up and hardened over time. I felt as if I had gone red all over but at the same time I was aware that, rather than intending serious harm, they wanted to offer a warning concealed in some sort of joke. A voice came to me from behind the veil which had gone back into place like a turkey cock's wattle:

'Why do you smoke? Isn't it wrong?'

I didn't cry out – I was too scared, and perhaps I thought it was more manly as well. But mostly it was fear that was the reason I kept my mouth shut while he asked me if I said my prayers like my father, who was renowned for his piety, and then I spoke when he increased the pressure: 'No.'

Harder still he pressed, and the question struck my ear like a quiet hot flame: 'Why?'

And I said: 'I will pray . . . I will', and found my body growing cooler and returning to life. But I had hardly begun to breathe freely again when I felt a hand coming down on my back like a butcher's chopper on a swollen carcase:

'No, I must say you're a brave lad. You'll be a credit to your father. If you'd been afraid I would have driven you into the ground there like an onion. Get up.'

What could I do? I stood up. 'Come here.'

I went.

'Listen.'

My ear, which still felt like a glowing coal in the darkness of the night, was proffered, and I listened and heard the Stranger, Abu Muhammad, clear his throat a little and say, 'I'm hungry, son.'

I swear that my heart never felt so light as it did at the sound of those words, which drove away all the night's fear and apprehension and settled deep down inside me. They began to echo through me, and set up curious and delightful impulses towards high-minded loving kindness, and an overwhelming desire for sacrifice, of which the easiest kind is of course self-sacrifice. Almost whispering, I said: 'What would you like to eat?'

'Anything. And if you can, bring me cigarettes and a battery and a pitcher of water.'

I turned to run but didn't move because he had grabbed hold of the tail of my gallabiyya and held on to it with those terrible fingers. I faced him again and found his veil lifted to speak:

'On your honour as a man?'

I scowled silently, miserable because I felt that he was insulting me. Perhaps the moonlight falling on my pale excited face warned him too that I was overwrought and almost crying, and he let go of me. But still I didn't go: I stood there unable to talk, wanting to tell him so many things but uncertain how to say them, probably because I couldn't even formulate them in my mind. I was also aware that the burst of enthusiasm that had flooded through me at his request was beginning to die away, and it crossed my mind that I could go and wake up my father and alert the night patrol and the village mayor and we could all go and capture him.

I stood there until he said:

'Go on . . . off you go.'

'Aren't you afraid of what I might do?'

In a calm controlled whisper which pierced right to the marrow of my bones, he ordered me, 'Get out', and in much confusion I began to feel my way along the path which led to our house nearby.

6

Whoever would have thought that I'd go back to him when I'd escaped with my skin? And who could have possibly believed that a lasting relationship would grow up between us? He even came to trust me so much that he made me responsible for his young wife Warda, the most beautiful and delectable woman I'd ever set eyes on.

Man must be the only living creature to rush headlong into danger, knowingly, and call it courage and glory in it, instead of instinctively fleeing from it like other animals. Otherwise no power in existence would have driven me back to the spot where I'd last seen the Stranger, carrying all the food I could lay hands on in our house, and the pitcher of water specially reserved for my father, which none of us normally dared touch.

That was the story of my first encounter with the Stranger and it turned out not to be the last. For many days I met him regularly taking him food and water and all the little things which he needed in order to be able to stay completely hidden. It wasn't an easy task since there was no food to be bought in the village, and it required a great deal of tricky manoeuvring to get some of it from our house and then to think up convincing reasons to persuade my relations to supply me with the rest.

At first the Stranger treated me with great caution. I never once went to him with the food and found him in the place where we'd agreed to meet. It was always empty and I would stand there wavering between doubt and fear until he emerged from some secret hiding place, after he had reassured himself that I was alone. I always met him at night, between sunset and the evening prayer. Despite my extreme youth and the unusual nature of the relationship he never asked me to keep what passed between us a secret – needless to say I would have died before disclosing it to anybody. How wonderful those days were when I was keeper of the Stranger's secret and his only link with the outside world.

I was aware all the time that at last, and in a way I couldn't have envisaged, I had entered the world which I had so long dreamt about. How happy I felt when we shared the food that I'd brought or sat together for longer than usual and talked. I did most of the talking, leaving the Stranger the job of encouraging me to keep going, or interrupting my incessant flow with a question – but how trivial the great events of my life seemed to me when I was describing them to him; the important fights and quarrels paled into insignificance when I told of them to a man who was known to kill at the slightest provocation, and sometimes with none at all.

It took many meetings and prolonged conversation before I really looked at him properly and became thoroughly familiar with his features. The most striking of them was his thick black moustache where a few stark white hairs had begun to appear: it spread across his face, dominating it and distracting attention from his sharp thin nose and his small eyes which had reddened lids and lashes that were partly eaten away. His hands were odd – tough and hard but smaller than mine were then, with shorter fingers, and his sandals were so small that they looked as if they'd been cut to fit a young boy or even a girl – and I remember noticing that he was no taller than me, possibly a little shorter. When he laughed he had a habit of adding a sort of rattle at the end, perhaps because he wanted to lend a certain harshness to his laughter.

After many nights I had reached the stage when I felt able to ask a question that, according to him, only a 'kid' like myself, or a madman, would have asked. Why did he choose to be a notorious killer rather than an ordinary God-fearing person – what had made him live the kind of life he did? He laughed, and rattled, and said: 'What kind of a question's that? Ask me another.'

But I, as if in a playful sort of way I were taking liberties a little with my father, kept on at him to answer me. At last, after much urging on my part, he began to look grave and abstracted; this went on for so long that I was afraid he was not trying to answer my question at all and was preoccupied with following some noise back to its source, for his ears were always alert to the slightest sound. Then he said, 'The truth is I don't really know. All I can tell you is that every time it was a case of kill or be killed.'

It already seemed to me with these high-sounding words that he had begun to reveal the secrets of the awesome world of night, and breathless with excitement I asked him, 'Kill or be killed? What do you mean?'

'I mean if I hadn't killed the other man, he would have killed me – so I killed him.'

'And that's how it happened every time?'

'Every time.'

'Even the first time?'

At this he was silent and looked serious again. Then he said:

'No. It's the first time that's difficult. I was working for

someone, on the land. He didn't pay me. I went to him asking
him for my wages three times, and I told people about it, and they
were all on my side; but he didn't give in. They told me to report
him to the authorities. I did, and they put *me* in prison and beat
me up. While I was inside I decided to kill him, and the very day I
got out, I sold my one small buffalo and bought a gun and shot
him outside his front door. I was interrogated and held but they
couldn't prove anything against me, so his family went and hired
someone to kill me in revenge. Was I going to wait for him to kill
me? I killed him and that was that. I've been doing it ever since.'

'But . . . I mean . . . that man – weren't you angry or anything
when you killed him?'

'I was angry all right. I'd been sitting there for a month without
eating or drinking. I was sick, and the only thing that cured me
was hearing that his family had hired someone to kill me.'

He was suddenly silent, and I felt uneasy. Then he turned to
me and said sharply:

'And why do you want to know about it?'

'The thing is, that I want to kill somebody.'

He laughed until the tears came into his eyes:

'Kill somebody? Who? Tell me, and I'll do it for you.'

'Nobody in particular. Just anybody.'

'Anybody? What do you mean, anybody?'

'Just anybody.'

It was very difficult to explain what I wanted to him, to
elucidate the details of my secret desire and its power over me:
how it had made me hang around Mr. Khalil and how I had
wanted to meet him for so long and had never dared to tell
anyone about it but him. He looked at me out of the corner of his
eye, and I discovered then that when he did this he squinted.

'Are you serious?'

'Of course I am – otherwise why would I be talking to you?'

'Why are you talking to me?'

'So that you can teach me how to kill.'

Again he laughed fit to burst and then, clapping me on the
back, he said:

'Don't you think it's wrong to talk like that? Teach you how to
kill? Do you think it's like learning to play cards, monsieur?'

I felt myself despised, especially at the use of the word

'monsieur', which he pronounced in an irritating way, dragging out each syllable. And he for some reason was the one person who I had thought would not mock me if ever I had the chance to tell him about it, let alone laugh at me like any casual acquaintance, or like one of my schoolmates. I didn't want to have a great struggle to convince him, only to have him taking it all as a joke, so I shut up.

Neither of us spoke for a while, then I felt him patting my shoulder as if he wanted to make friends again.

'If you want to kill somebody, we'll manage it. It's simple enough.'

Hope flooded back to me:

'You promise?'

'On one condition. If I ask you to run an errand for me, will you do it?'

'Anything you like.'

7

Up till then I had never considered the Stranger as a human being like the rest of us, part of a family perhaps, with a mother and father or a wife – or several wives. But he didn't give me time to wonder or express astonishment, just hurried on to explain the details of my mission: I had to deliver a five-pound note to his first wife and bring the second one to him.

The first lived in a village close to ours. She was brown as an old bird, brown and dried-up and skinny, like the branch of a withered acacia tree. She had at least ten children, all of them brown and dried-up like her, and she drove me nearly out of my head as she cross-examined me, asking me all manner of details about him, obviously full of misgivings, and I heaved a sigh of relief when the whole thing was over and she let me go.

After that I had to go to Warda, his latest wife, unimaginably soft and feminine and beautiful. I'd never visited the estate which the Stranger described to me but I knew that it lay beyond the pumping station where the water level in the big drainage canal was raised to the level of the lake. I chose to go in the late afternoon so that I could bring her back in the dark. I was nervous and afraid, and felt sure that everybody I passed must recognize me and identify the 'token' which the Stranger had provided me with for the purpose of reassuring Warda that I was genuine. What a token it was – a black eyebrow pencil that she had asked him to get for her. Somehow I couldn't accept that the Stranger would stoop to mention such a thing, let alone concern himself enough actually to remember that she wanted it.

When I arrived at the farmstead it was still empty except for the old women and the children. I was welcomed by a dreadful storm of barking from a bunch of skinny dogs that looked half-dead with hunger. They wouldn't leave me alone and I would have turned round and gone home, had it not been for a large peasant woman with mud-stained clothes who appeared in the nick of time and fended them off and led me to Warda's house.

On her own initiative she volunteered a justification for my visit: 'You'll be one of her relations from the station.' This was what people used to call the capital of the province because the railway was there. She also knocked on Warda's door for me with her work-stained hand and called out to her to open it for the guests. From inside a voice answered her: it had a joyful melodious note to it, yet it was a city voice whose sweet refinement sounded incongruous and strange in that remote uncouth spot buried deep in the countryside.

The door opened and for a split second I caught a glimpse of the most beautiful face that I had ever set eyes on. The skin was so fair that it seemed almost translucent, her features so perfect that she looked like the women in the pictures on boxes of Turkish delight. It was obvious that she had just finished bathing, and she had only combed out part of her wet hair. For a second I glimpsed her before she withdrew instinctively behind the door, and re-emerged with a gallabiyya draped over her, covering her hair, and failing to cover her face. Still I saw no more because my head dropped forward on to my chest in embarrassment, and I did not raise my eyes from the ground, and almost ordered my ears not to listen when I heard Warda's voice with the joyful gentle trilling note lurking within it, bidding me welcome, inviting me in, although she could not yet have known who I was or why I had come.

I became more and more embarrassed and tongue-tied as I

explained to her as quickly and in as few words as possible, and my ears burned and grew hot when I mentioned the 'token'. But regardless of the things I said, her tone of voice didn't alter and she continued in the same vein, welcoming me and inviting me to sit down. When I hesitated she took my hand in her soft one that was still damp from her bath and pulled me inside: 'In you come, sweetheart. Think of it as your home. Please come in. Please do.'

She didn't let go of me till she had led me to an inner room, furnished for receiving guests, and with her free hand had reached for a splendidly patterned rug, spread it out and put two cushions on it – one for me to sit on, the other to lean against, as she insisted.

I had hardly had time to draw breath before she had brought in the tea things and made tea; when she handed me a glass of it, it made the soft whiteness of her hand appear reddish. Then she asked me what I thought of it, and said she had taken care to make it weak so that it would be suitable for a 'gentleman' like me.

With the first few sips of tea I began to come to my senses. Up till then she had been bustling around so busily, being hospitable and making me welcome, that I'd had no chance to talk about why I'd come, or even to mention anything about the nature of my relationship with her husband. The longer I was there, the more attentive she became towards me and in my confusion I began to think desperately how to put my glass down and prepare myself to deliver the message to her. But before I could act she had moved much closer to me: 'Why are you shy, sweetheart? Don't you feel at home here? Aren't we good enough for you? Don't be shy, little brother, please don't be shy.'

Then she rocked me gently to and fro drawing me right up close to her.

I would have recovered my composure had I not glanced up at her. She was treating me like a schoolboy even though she was only a few years older than me herself; but the age difference was immaterial and what counted was that she was a woman and I was a hoarse-voiced adolescent with a sticking-out Adam's apple. Not only was she young, but unbearably beautiful – fair-skinned and lovely, enclosed in her tight silk dress, her breasts and stomach and thighs blossoming and thrusting against it. Even had she had the body of a man, the beautiful darkness in her eyes was enough to evoke desires so palpable and compelling that they almost announced themselves with loud cries. None of this seemed to inhibit her at all; she caressed me, put her arm round me, and every time I lowered my eyes and looked away insisted on turning my face towards her again. She offered me cigarettes, tobacco, anything I wanted, and stroked my hair remarking: 'You've got beautiful golden hair, like an Englishman's. God bless you, little brother.'

When she said 'little brother', it made me tremble, and the sentiments expressed were far from sisterly.

All this time I was agitated by my knowledge that in spite of the way she was behaving, she was the wife of the mighty Stranger who was crouched waiting for our return with his knife strapped to his left leg. My nerves reached breaking-point when she started tapping me on the shoulder from time to time coquettishly, and said: 'Don't be like that. You know what it's all about already. There must be lots of girls after you with that hair of yours. You're lovely. Stay the night here, won't you? I won't let you go all by yourself.'

A great feeling of irritation surged over me: the irritation of one delegated to perform a duty who finds that he himself has become the object of dutiful ministrations. My mission was quite lost sight of in the dreadful hubbub of welcome, the continuous personal questions, and the caresses and embraces − on the surface expressions of unadulterated affection − which made my head spin.

From time to time I sprang to my feet as if I were about to run off, but immediately her arm was around me, holding me down. She would touch my hair with a kiss that sent shivers down my spine, and ask me playfully why I was in such a hurry. As if I were an unreasoning toy with no mind of my own, she touched me, my face and the stubble on my chin and my sprouting moustache, with her electric fingers, and I sat in mounting anger. I commanded myself never for one moment to lose sight of the image of the Stranger which I kept between me and this woman with her city ways, who seemed not to know the restraints of shyness and embarrassment. She acted like a woman who had never been with a man in her life before, and I wondered what he was doing with her, since it was obvious that she didn't give him a thought, and felt no fear of him.

Perhaps a combination of annoyance and disgust, and the strangeness of the whole situation, made me suddenly feel tremendous contempt for Warda, despite her extraordinary beauty and the overwhelming force of her personality. The Stranger was far away and other men who would have come to her were frightened for their lives, and in the exile of her enforced celibacy the chance that had driven me into her path had provided her with a last resort. Who did she think she was, and what did she take me for, the whore?

Just like that, with a great onrush of revulsion, I freed myself; then I was able to stare fixedly at her, without a trace of embarrassment or confusion, and deliver the message word for word. She seemed dumbfounded by the change in me and her eyes, suddenly full of confusion, flickered uncertainly. But this only lasted for a second and then a gleam of sorts came back to them. It didn't take much intelligence to realize that she had interpreted my withdrawal and my obvious distaste as a sign that her feminine charms had failed with me, and that to succeed she must sharpen her weapons and return to the fray. This time her embraces were shameless, although she insisted on prefacing each one with a pious imprecation: 'God bless you; the Prophet keep you.' My disgust became overt and it was her turn to be embarrassed. Eventually she asked:

'Don't you find me attractive?'

At this point I found myself shouting at her: 'What's the matter with us both? I was sent by the Stranger – your husband. Are you coming or not?'

She seemed to read in my eyes that there would be no retrieving the situation, but she didn't withdraw straight away. She kept talking, as if to work out my latest reaction to her, and heal the rift. In the end she said that I would have to go back and tell the Stranger that she couldn't come to him; when I asked her why she refused to say, and begged me simply to tell him what she had said and not to add any comments of my own. After a pause, she said, 'If he wants to see me, let him come here', and both of us realized, as she spoke, that this was absurd, for his coming to her would mean certain danger.

When I could no longer see any benefit to be gained from staying I hurried to leave, but she caught hold of me, and made me stay until she had stuffed my pockets full of pastries; she had rolled them up in a magazine cover, and insisted that I take them with me. When I was halfway home I took them out and tried to bite one of them but it stuck in my throat, and I hurled it with all my strength into the canal; then solemnly I pictured to myself what it would be like when I came face to face with the Stranger.

8

Our meeting was sad, I don't know why. I felt as if I'd failed in the task he'd entrusted to me, and that complications had arisen in my simple clear-cut relationship with him. To me he had been an innocent hero with no ties binding him to the kind of life that we all lived, then I had discovered, unexpectedly, that he had a wife – and one like Warda. Somehow this made me feel ashamed, as if it should have been my duty not to find out, and I had caught him in a moment of weakness, in a situation where his honour was questionable.

All he did when he saw me was to say: 'Ah . . . she didn't come?' and for the first time in my dealings with him I realized that, in order to be able to answer him, I would have to lie, and I tried to look for excuses for her. But he just nodded and said: 'All right . . . it doesn't matter. Did anyone see you going there?'

From his despondent tone I could tell that he just wanted to change the subject and it irritated me that he didn't flare up at me and go for my throat, or else start off at once for the estate where Warda lived and tear her from her bed and carry her off. Even when I tried to return to the subject, secretly disapproving of the whole situation, he didn't appear to be annoyed, and began to ask after her – was she well? what exactly was she doing when I arrived ? – as if he were making a great effort to behave like any other husband temporarily separated from his wife. Be that as it may, each one of his questions produced a cold sweat from my armpits, as I wondered if he knew that my answer did not tell the whole story, and I couldn't begin to breathe freely again until he nodded his head and passed on to another question.

Till this day I can remember how he suddenly looked up, his grizzled head showing all of his fifty years, the characteristic narrowness of his eyes hidden by the darkness, so that they appeared no more than shadowy circles on either side of his nose. His silence washed over me and I began to grow uneasy and tried desperately to discern, behind the dark glasses of night on his eyes, what it was that he wanted from me. Suddenly he said, 'Listen, monsieur'; but sheer terror prevented me from prompting him to go on or even assuming an attentive attitude.

The moon looked down on us from far away, high up above the trees crouched in the darkness and the great eucalyptuses bordering the field on our right, like a broken milk pitcher left on a saint's tomb to await a blessing. Its faint light glowed reddish like a paraffin lamp deprived of air and the Stranger's head appeared monstrous, out of all proportion to the rest of his body, staring dumb and heavy like a dead head. From lips that hardly moved his voice reached me: 'Why are you lying to me, monsieur?'

I died, falling off the edge of the world into the yawning chasm of the hereafter: my heart stopped, my mind was paralyzed, my limbs froze and my skin excreted its fear in tiny beads of sweat which gathered and grew. Grabbing desperately at the void, I repeated foolishly: 'Why?'

Again his voice came to me, the voice of the darkness if darkness could speak: 'Why are you lying to me, monsieur?'

I swallowed, trying to suppress the noise I made, and before I could try again to speak he said: 'Did you do anything with Warda?'

He must have noticed me straightening up as if stung, and he rephrased his question: 'Or did she mess about with you, monsieur?'

In the fraction of a second that followed, I made up my mind to let down my defences and tell him everything, and if I escaped with my skin, to sever my connection with both of them; I had no part in these problems – I had involved myself in them because of a childish whim, and looked likely to lose my life for it. But then I was knocked sideways by the onrush of life returning when the unexpected, the extraordinary happened – the Stranger emitted a huge thunderous laugh and the shadows of the night were scattered, and my mind unloosed from its moorings. His short powerful hand reached out to pat me on the shoulder and he spoke, this time in the voice of the light if light could speak, his features mobile and expressive as life flooded back to them:

'You were afraid, weren't you, monsieur? It's not fair to tease you like that. Tell me then – what did she do to you?'

How could I have known that his new wife's behaviour was no secret to him? She was his favourite, the apple of his eye, and he had taken her in the full knowledge of her weakness. He had seen her singing at weddings with a troupe of musicians and had fallen madly in love with her, and then married her – more or less by force. Then he'd put her on this out-of-the-way estate, like a bird in an open cage, to taunt other men. But she taunted him as much and, according to Khalil, who told me the whole story, they were like the woman and the genie in 'A Thousand and One Nights': the genie put the woman in a bottle and kept the key, while she had a bag full of the rings given to her by the men she had betrayed him with, despite the sealed bottle and the awe that his brute strength inspired. Of course, Warda had no bag of rings, and the Stranger was palpably more influential than the genie, and loved more. He was mean with himself and his other wives and his children so that he could lavish things on her, and he didn't ask her to be faithful to him or even to observe the conventions of respectable behaviour, saying to her, apparently: 'If you get the opportunity to do something, you'll be within your rights.'

Perhaps he had no alternative, and wanted to be able to justify her wrongdoing to himself if necessary. And all the time the fires of doubt ate away at his soul, tormenting him, and the question nagged at him, sapping his strength: had she seen her chance and taken it, or remained ensnared, unable to stray because of the dread which his name could still evoke?

Whenever his lack of faith in her and his self-doubt reached a certain pitch, he felt driven to make a show of strength to convince himself and others that he was still in charge: he would strike out violently, unleashing his fury on the immediate neighbourhood and on all the surrounding countryside, making his name into a more terrible deterrent than ever the genie's bottle was.

How was I to have known that he had chosen me simply as live bait to tempt her with, to show her that although he was far away he was capable of paralyzing my will and using me to make a fool of her? Warda must have known that sooner or later I would break down and tell him everything, so that her behaviour with me had been calculated precisely with that in mind, to reply to his challenge and challenge him in return. I had been a living letter sent by the Stranger to inquire after his wife's state of mind and gauge the extent of her submission to him. She had written her reply on the same paper, full of rebellion against him. He had sent me to prove to her that his influence over me was far more powerful than all her beauty and feminine charms, while she had tried to prove that the opposite was true.

But that night all that the Stranger did while I was telling him what had happened, was to listen to me, laughing from time to time, not in his usual raucous way but like an adolescent boy pleased with himself and his virility.

When I had finished talking he said to me with some seriousness:

'Okay, monsieur, if she was your wife and behaved like that what would you do with her?'

With genuine anger I replied: 'I would have killed her ages ago.'

'Just like that? Is it so easy to kill someone?'

'For you it must be anyway.'

He bowed his head again: 'Killing people is one thing and killing your wife is another. Who knows . . . it seems to me that everyone I meet has thought about killing his wife, but the trouble is you can never finally decide one way or the other. One day you'll say to yourself, "that's it, there's no hope for her, let's kill her," then the next day you might find yourself saying, "give her a chance, she might improve . . ." and you go on like that, alternating between the two, for the rest of your life. If it was that easy to decide, everyone would have killed his wife at least once in his lifetime.'

I didn't understand exactly what he was getting at, but I realized that he wasn't being straight with me, which was uncharacteristic, and that for the first time I was seeing him making light of something that mattered desperately to him. So I said; 'But I always thought you weren't like that.'

He raised his head a little, and half-jokingly, half-serious said: 'Soon you'll be grown up, then you'll know what I mean.'

I noticed how his neck drooped and his head hung like a listless uncertain flag and I almost pitied him. I was tired of him and bored of sitting there with him, and I got up to go. Suddenly he leapt to his feet and listened, and he seemd to prick up his ears like a dog sensing danger. Then he spoke, panting slightly as if he'd been running: 'Take your robe in your teeth and fly for your life. Don't stop till you reach home.'

9

I spent the night turning this way and that in a hidden fever of anxiety, wondering why he'd ordered me to run, or going back over the conversation we'd had, trying to reconcile the picture of the Stranger that I'd constructed for myself with the view I'd formed of him since I'd met him: a dominating figure and yet strangely weak; a man who terrorized the world but did not frighten Warda, the person who should have been more terrified of him than anyone else. He meanwhile was spending one of the most miserable nights of his life, as I was to learn the following day.

His senses had been accurate: an enlarged patrol with the commissioner himself at its head had been out searching for him in those very fields. If we had talked for just a few moments longer they would have been upon us – or if his hearing had been less sharp.

The following night I took him the water melon that he had mentioned having a longing for. I split it open to let it get cool and then sat waiting for him. After a long time he still hadn't appeared, and I contented myself with devouring what I could of the melon and burying the rest in the ground. I went home, not knowing whether to rejoice or be cast down at the breaking of the thread that had bound me to him. Although I had known him for such a short time this had been enough to take the edge off my appetite, but on the other hand it had not achieved what I had wanted it to – he had not taught me to kill as I had dreamt he would, and I had almost come to believe that he himself didn't know how to.

A few days went by, perhaps two, perhaps three, and then one night I awoke to a muffled crack resounding against the wall by my bed. I was wide awake by then, listening hard and, more clearly this time, there came another crack, the sound of a small pebble which I was certain had been thrown at my window deliberately to attract my attention. I wondered who it could be, as the Stranger didn't know exactly which house was ours, and even if he'd found out, how would he have known which was my room and which window was nearest to where I slept?

I sat up, extreme apprehension making my mind go blank, so that my head resounded like an empty tin to the smallest movement or the most fleeting thought. I opened the window cautiously and from the semi-darkness outside the house I heard a whispered command: 'Come down.' Then another: 'And bring the Italian.'

The words gleamed in the darkness like a sharp knife blade, then disappeared. Everything retreated into shadowy stillness almost as it had been before, except I noticed the darkest, stillest spot moving, taking on human form, and going off towards the fields.

My delight overcame everything else – my nervousness and my fears that someone else in the house might have been woken too – my father I thought of especially since he was roused by the slightest sound. Waves of happiness swept over me as I groped my way to the shed below the pigeon-house where I'd hidden the small Italian sub-machinegun that the Stranger had given me. During the few days when I hadn't seen him my life had begun to return to normal – trivial, uneventful, empty of secrecy and night. How vastly different it had seemed; how often I'd wandered through the corn hoping that perhaps I might pick up the thread that would lead me back to him. And now he had come back of his own accord, and in a way that set my imagination on fire.

My joy overcame my misgivings, and in no time I was standing in front of him in the place where we always used to meet, panting, telling him about the melon, handing him the gun and loading it in front of him as he had taught me. When I had calmed down and began to look at him, I realized to my confusion that he was not as he had been. He said nothing – he had drawn himself in and gathered up his resources to concentrate his will on one small defined area. He had an expression that I hadn't seen him wear before, of passionate involvement, madness even, and a new spirit moved through him, which silenced my chatter all at once, and made me adopt the position of a soldier awaiting orders from his superior. Sure enough, I found him saying, urgently: 'Are you going home or coming with me?'

Quickly I replied: 'I'll come with you ... but where are we going?'

'Don't ask. Perhaps we're going to kill someone. Perhaps we'll be killed. Are you coming?'

Without waiting for an answer he parted the corn stalks and his short figure disappeared.

After a moment's hesitation I followed him.

10

I made no more attempts to drag conversation out of him; he was like one bound to a distant goal which drew him along, blinding him to his surroundings and not allowing him time to pause or speak. He led me over bridges, skirted canals and crawled on his hands along the bottoms of flood basins, not seeing me or hearing me, for all practical purposes unaware of my existence. On the rare occasions when he did speak, it was no more than: 'What ... what did you say?', and when I tried to ask him a question he mumbled something, and I realized that he was deep in thought and it was no use trying to extract an answer from him.

The night was big and frightening like a funeral tent crowned with black, in mourning for the death of day, and only the pale moon and the stars were lit to guide the mourners. The fields were wide and vast, wider than the fields of day; cut wheat gave way to standing corn, and maize to cotton, and we watched our dim reflections in the water which submerged the earth in expectation of the rice-planting. Land and more land, as far as the eye could see, every inch of it cultivated and cared for. Those poor creatures lying in their beds sweated for it, and then slept as if from sadness, tossing and turning, waiting for the day to come and scoop them up in its grasp and scatter them over the face of the earth; then they would turn its dark wastelands into green and its clay to bread until night came and cut them down and stored them safe away from its secrets in their human storehouses themselves made from the soil.

What a gulf separated us from them – those who lived off the land, and then returned to it to nourish its life with their bones. They slept now in their far-off homes, content with their complete submission to existence, to the inexorability of heaven and earth, the unchanging limits of day and night; and we passed through their world, cavalier with their efforts to exploit it and embellish it. The Stranger walking ahead of me, with his small hands and powerful arms, had struggled to escape from the grasp of day and night's dispassionate cutting down, and sought to make them yield to laws of his own making. He wanted this power to be evident to people so that they would fear him as they feared God, and the next world, and the winter's bitterest cold. From behind, I considered his smallness – even with the gun slung over his shoulder – and the enormity of the night, and it seemed to me that he was much too frail to take hold of its reins and become its master.

But we were not alone out there. I heard him mumbling indistinctly, then, more clearly, greeting someone. I looked around me and could just make out two men or more who had taken refuge from the night under a bridge, or perhaps it was in the shadow of a water-wheel. Rather than wondering what they were doing there, why they too had left their beds to hold silent counsel in the pitch blackness in this dreary spot, I knew with a shudder, and an involuntary nod of my head, that they were Sons of the Night, aspiring to the same way of life as the Stranger; when they heard his greeting they felt safe, and returned it, as if exchanging a password. And they had not abandoned their peasant hospitality, for they went on, 'Please join us'; to my immense delight extending their invitation to me when they had registered my presence.

Gradually, after long exposure to the night as we plunged deeper into its darkness, I began to see the Stranger with new eyes. My vision suffused with the night that surrounded us, I was able to sense how he was at one with it. It became impossible to imagine it without him, or to conceive of life for him and others like him outside the protection of its sheltering arms. These strangers shunned the unambiguous paternity of daytime and took refuge with their undeclared father, the night. The anonymity of it attracted them, and they hated the day with its clarity and legality. Anyone who witnessed their intimacy with it and their acclimatization to its wildness, would be forced to conclude that there would always be people like them, even if the whole earth was built over. As long as the night keeps its irresistible magic, who can blame them, since it has lured them away from the day and made them what they are? The night will continue to bring forth its own for as long as water brings forth fish, deserts herdsmen, and exile a yearning for home.

There have always been men like him, and always will be, despite the fact that down the ages they have been subjected to the severest punishments, and have perished. Every time one of them is lost, the night claims another from the day, perhaps so that the wheel keeps turning and there are always two distinct worlds, day and night – although those that live in the day are always the majority – perhaps even to ensure that we have a choice, and, whichever world we live in, it is of our own free will.

Suddenly the Stranger put an arm out to stop me, and I found myself face to face with him, and he began to examine me. At this point I asked myself what was preventing a man like that from killing me: we were in a remote place, the impassive night was our only witness, and, if he needed a pretext, what had happened between me and Warda was sufficient. The only thing I could think of was that he knew me, and that now there was enough of a bond between us to afford me some reassurance. Who knows, perhaps if the mutual knowledge between people was firm enough they would not venture to kill each other, and fear between them would be non-existent. Such thoughts were going through my head when he spoke, in a voice hoarse from the long silence and the dampness of the dew:

'Are you afraid?'

'No.'

'Ready for anything?'

'What sort of thing?'

He didn't answer. Once again he looked closely at me, and then said: 'Can you see that fire?'

I hadn't noticed it but when I peered about I could see a distant glowing spot, like a one-eyed wolf's eye, that could have been embers.

'Do you know who's over there?'

'Who?'

'Shalabi.'

'Who's Shalabi?'

'My friend, my dear friend. I'm going to see him. It's been so long, and I've missed him with all my heart.'

Then he explained to me my part in the proceedings; he wanted me to give Shalabi and the man with him a fright – they were sitting by the fire roasting corn on the cob, and the smell of it filled the air. I had to creep up to them with the gun, then jump out at them shouting, 'What are you doing here, you bastards?' at which point, he assured me, he would show himself, we would all laugh at what had happened, and then we would sit down with them to roast corn and eat it.

I must confess I felt as if I were going to my doom; my heart wouldn't stop beating and the gun trembled in my hand until I was forced to hold it with both hands and press it against my shoulder. Very slowly, I moved forward, and it seemed to take a lifetime before I had covered enough ground to be able to see their faces. One of them was young and handsome with a woollen skull-cap worn at a rakish angle, and the other was obviously an official night-watchman; he sat cross-legged, his gun across his knees, and poked the fire, and blew on it, while the young man sat hugging his knees, his face thoughtful.

If I hadn't been afraid of the Stranger I would have fired in the air over their heads. A loaded gun in my hand was a great temptation, and firing from a distance would have been much easier than confronting the two men.

I stood there hesitant and trembling, until I saw the figure of the Stranger emerging from the doorway of the barn behind them, and at that moment, as if I'd received an unspoken order, I shot forward suddenly, like a mad bull, bellowing, covering the distance between myself and them in a series of wild leaps. In no time I was in front of them, separated from them only by the fire's pale embers. I pointed the gun at them with a ridiculously exaggerated gesture, but the trick was far more successful than I'd anticipated: they sprang backwards in genuine alarm and the watchman started to shout as if he'd gone out of his mind. In retrospect all this has been swamped, engulfed as if it had never been, by the other events that started up at approximately the same time, the most dreadful, shocking spectacle I have ever witnessed in my life.

I had no choice but to look; and to this moment I can remember how the Stranger moved closer until he was right up behind them, then raised his hands high above his head – whether I actually saw him bringing them down again, I can't say, but what I remember next is a noise, unlike any I had heard before, any other in existence. One egg smashing another, if an egg was the size of a human head. Hot metal hissing in water. That's what I remember, noise, and then the rakish youth half rising to his feet, but not sitting down again. One of his feet went up in the air, then descended in jerks at regular intervals, like the second hand of a watch. His head dropped too, not the same head I had seen as I came towards them, but an indistinct mass split by a black shining thing; and it may unnerve even the most stoical to learn that it was an axe that had gone straight down through one eye to the cheek bone.

11

The whole operation didn't last more than a few seconds but it took up years of my life going back over it and thinking about it. On each occasion the same feelings of nausea swept over me, the same convulsive shudderings, as if I were the one whose skull had been split.

There is some powerful force in us that makes us suffer when we see another suffer and almost die at another's dying. There had been no ties joining me and the young man, yet his violent death haunted me, and I was tormented not just by fellow-feeling for the victim, but worse than that, by a sense of identification with the killer.

My terror in the few minutes that followed his death was if anything more acute than at the moment of death. The Stranger's face was dreadful to behold when he pulled out the axe, horribly embedded, and stood leaning on it, panting. He glanced from me to the watchman who lay sprawled on the ground, either unconscious or dead from fear. The fire's glow lit up the Stranger's face lending substance to the misgivings expressed there, and I was no longer able to control my suppressed shudders, which gave way to an audible shivering.

I had never seen his small eyes so large; I didn't think that human eyes had it in them to become so round and widen so, and I fancied that even if he had been the dead man himself fear would not have struck such terror into his eyes nor death made his face so pale. It was as if the blow which had split the man's head in two had opened a secret door out of which had come some evil demon who himself wielded an axe and menaced the Stranger's own skull. Only such an apparition would seem to account for his bulging eyes and his sudden loss of self-awareness, as he began to move with rapid crazed movements, looking about him, twisting and turning, lashing out with the axe, a different man from the one that had gone with me through the night.

Now, I felt, he could easily have buried his axe in my head without provocation, or cut the watchman in two where he lay. He was clearly capable of anything in his unreasoning state and there would have been no stopping him if he had embarked on an orgy of death and destruction supposedly defending himself against the monster which stood there in front of him scaring him out of his wits.

The watchman and I escaped by some miracle that night, and as it was I almost felt driven to pull the trigger as he had shown me how, and keep it there till I'd emptied the gun into him. We were all equally frightened, the professional killer no less than the foolhardy novice, and bent on self-preservation; I clung to the gun, he to the axe searching desperately like a madman for the thing which haunts him, while the watchman held fast to his faint, seeking protection in unconsciousness. It was as if even the dead man would have chosen to stay where he was, preferring a thousand times to die once only than to return to life to face death from the axe again. The fire blazed away, resisting extinction by burning up corn-cobs, and they resisted the fire, fear of their fate making them fizzle and hiss, and cracked from time to time, crying out to the fire for mercy with the last spark of life left in them. All-embracing fear of death existed side by side with a stubborn clinging on to life, and the right to self-defence, while the night grew darker in a final attempt to stand against the rising day, and the only impartial spectator was the snub-nosed moon, choked with pity for us, apparently sad in the fact of destiny.

And then we began to smell human flesh roasting, mixing with the smell of roasted corn and filling the air.

Suddenly we started to move. A blow from the Stranger's foot set the watchman on his feet again, and then the two men together lifted the dead man and put out the fire which had begun spreading to his clothes and the flesh on his arm. I took the gun and the axe and they went ahead of me with their burden. We didn't go far – after a few yards we came to an abandoned water-wheel, of the kind which was once used to draw water from underground when the Nile was low. Grass had begun to grow all around it, and its water had become stagnant, metallic and oily; already it had fallen into their hands and they used it as a meeting-place, and a cache for stolen goods, but till then I hadn't known that it served as a grave for those whom it would have been inappropriate to bury more conventionally. A stone was tied to the body before it was thrown in, and the water took care of it and its clothes in a matter of days.

We returned in silent procession; this time I was at the front, the watchman in the middle and the Stranger at the back, with the gun and the axe which I'd handed over to him. The watchman soon disappeared, after the Stranger and he had exchanged a few whispered words, and we went on our way alone.

For a while neither of us spoke, and then the Stranger began in an ordinary voice to apologize for having been forced to involve me in this dangerous game; he had had to kill Shalabi and there had been no one else available to help him.

Then he began to tell me about Shalabi – he had not been just his helper or a member of his gang, but his dearest friend. Their friendship had begun with a quarrel in the Wednesday market and had lasted ten years. He would have given him all that he had – himself, his name, his worldly goods – never doubting his sincerity right up to the day when they had arranged to meet at that same water-wheel where we had left him a few moments before. When he arrived he had found himself surrounded, a revolver at his head and fifty police marksmen covering him. Even when he was bundled into the truck and Shalabi was left behind, he never doubted him. How could he have guessed that all those years he had been eaten up with envy, that he had plotted continually to do away with him and take his place at the head of the gang and – what mattered much more to the Stranger – in Warda's bed? And yet it was Shalabi who had actually taken the initiative and made contact with the commissioner and organized the ambush with him.

He didn't tell it like a story, more as if he were exposing a wound that was still bleeding and hurting him, and once he fell silent, then suddenly, in great agitation, said 'The cap he was wearing the night of the ambush by the water-wheel, it was mine. I bought it off a stall for two pounds and he liked it, so I let him take it.' Then he laughed and said, 'If you want to know the truth, it wasn't his fault, it was mine. If I expect loyalty and friendship, I'm in the wrong job. In the night it's every man for himself and if you trust your neck to someone else you can't blame him for what happens.'

Then he turned to me and recounted how he had planned to kill Shalabi, just as Shalabi had planned to hand him over, more or less in the same venue, and with the same weapons – friendship and trust. The watchman came from the estate where Warda lived and Shalabi had been quick to befriend him and shower him with favours, so that he could hang around Warda with impunity. That very night they had planned to smuggle her out and had been awaiting the arrival of two other men with the means to put the plan into operation. Of course, Shalabi could have had no idea that the watchman had sold his secret, while for the watchman too the culmination of the action was quite unforeseen.

Although I was following what the Stranger was saying, at the same time a sly thought kept running through my head: what would my father say if he could see me now – he who never failed to perform every prayer enjoined upon him by religion? How would he have reacted if he had known what I had just witnessed and whose acolyte I had become, the man who with his talk plunged me deep into that odd abnormal world where I gleaned information of which even the most trivial details were enough to make your hair stand on end?

This may have distracted me from my surroundings, for I never noticed that all the time we had been close to the estate where Warda lived and that we had arrived more or less on her doorstep. The Stranger pulled at my gallabiyya to attract my attention: 'Look at this. It's blood, isn't it?'

When I looked closely I could see drops of blood on his hand and when he touched his thigh again there was more blood. He drew back his clothes and there was an ugly wound as if some mad creature had mauled him. One of the blows of the axe must have misfired and hit him when he was doing away with Shalabi.

12

The wound healed, of course, thanks to a certain Dr Ma'ruf who had learnt medicine by practising it. He was nominally a barber, but his fame as a surgeon had spread far and wide and they used to say that his lean hands, gentle and delicate as a woman's, did more to cure their ills than any real doctor's.

The story of the cure and my part in it would make up a novel by itself, but suffice it to say that it took place under the swing bridge where we decided to stay until his leg healed. I would never have imagined that it could be so spacious and so secure under there, that it was possible for a man to live there for several months without the people passing overhead knowing anything about it. Even more unexpected it became something enjoyable, a new exciting experience; you felt, as you moved about with your head bent, as if you were supporting the bridge on your shoulders, and it was strange to feel the water running beside you, at the foot of a small incline, and to hear a mixture of sounds as the earth and the iron bridge resounded to passing footsteps, and the water murmured its gentle tune.

I spent many days with him there, cut off from my family and

the outside world, as if I'd never known any other life. This state
of affairs had come about spontaneously, without any deliberate
decision on my part, but the Stranger's recovery was all that concerned me, my reason for living. We grew closer at that time, and
I could observe the contradictions in him at close hand: weakness
and strength existed side by side in him; he had strength of mind
and body in huge proportions, and yet he was vulnerable and
capable of suffering; he spoke rarely but was a master of epigram;
and of the great fund of information that he must have possessed,
he disclosed but little.

One memory from his convalescence has always stayed with
me vividly. Dr Ma'ruf was preparing to give him a pain-killing
injection when, as I looked at him, the colour drained away from
his face, he began to sweat, and his eyes grew wide as he glanced
desperately around him.

At first I didn't understand his behaviour and thought it must
be symptomatic of complications brought on by his injury. But
then Ma'ruf asked him, 'Are you frightened, or what?' which he
instantly denied with great force; and from this I concluded,
although I could hardly bring myself to believe it, that the
Stranger, the terrible, the feared, with his aura of inviolability,
was frightened of the needle, like any child. When Ma'ruf tried to
stick it in him, he begged him to wait a little, then shouted at him
demanding him to let him have time to catch his breath.
Eventually he weakeneed enough to try running away, moving
rapidly backwards until he was brought sharply to a halt by the
wall of the bridge. At that point Ma'ruf resorted to force, taking a
firm hold of his flesh and plunging the needle into it. A change
came over him then, and he was like a madman, or a cat in an
advanced state of terror, ready to lash out with his teeth and
claws. It brought back dramatically to me how he had been after
he killed Shalabi: his eyes grew inhumanly wide and smouldered
in defensive fear, and he was deathly pale right up to his
fingertips, again just as if he'd seen a dreadful apparition coming
to destroy him. It was an ugly moment that came to a head when
the Stranger swung round to Ma'ruf after he'd taken the needle
out, in a half-crazed way, and I thought he was about to grab him
by the throat and strangle him. Instead the action hung there, in
suspended animation, and the image of it was reflected in the

water running by us, like a lasting tableau trembling with the motion of the waves, of a man turned by fear into a wild animal.

Once when the pain had eased off temporarily, I discussed Warda with him. I had had more to do with her by then, and had come to despise her utterly and, inevitably, to despise him as a result. When I complained about her, he would nod his head, but in the manner of one who is not much concerned with the subject. I couldn't stomach seeing a man as urbane and experienced as him persist in trying to get a woman like her, who was unworthy of him, and had a complete disregard for his authority.

He was lying there keeping the flies off with a fly-swat that I'd made for him out of palm leaves. He closed his eyes and I felt that it was because he was embarrassed and ashamed and couldn't find the words to justify his position. What could he have said? It was obvious that she didn't attach any importance to her relationship with him and paid no attention to his letters and his requests. The one time she had visited him under the bridge was after much insisting on my part and expressly for my sake – and if only he'd known what it cost me. He kept his eyes shut for a long time, and when he opened them at last he said that that was it, he'd decided to finish with her; he would divorce her and let her go her own way. But I knew from the way he said 'he'd decided', that although perhaps he was sincere in his intention, his decision would never go beyond words.

Why did a man like him with his prestige and power persist in hanging on to a woman like Warda? Was it love, like they said, or was it living proof that there were areas where he was powerless, that he too had his limits, the same as any man?

The decision, in fact, came from her: when I went to her the next day, she wasn't there, and the neighbours said that she had taken her clothes, and all her things, and gone. Where to, nobody knew.

With childish enthusiasm I told him the news, not thinking for a moment of the effect it might have on him; never imagining that some hours afterwards, I would look at him and find real tears in his eyes.

But to get back to the story – the wound was on the way to recovery, the smell of it began to be bearable, and the Stranger regained his self-possession to some extent, and was able to amuse himself by doing a bit of fishing during the day. Meanwhile I deliberated over a certain matter and waited for the night to come before I faced him with it: I'd cast a critical eye over the state of my own life, and concluded that I was dancing on the stairs, neither going up nor coming down, neither becoming one of the Stranger's men nor going back to my everyday existence. I'd left home without a backward glance, and attached myself to the Stranger in pursuit of my dreams, but all that had happened was that both real life and my dreams had drifted away from me, and I was just acting as a sort of servant. I'd made my decision and waited impatiently for the right moment to disclose it to him.

At last, after much tedious waiting, night came, and scarcely had our evening meal finished, and darkness settled over everything, than I asked him if I could talk to him. He realized instinctively that it was something I could bear no longer so he listened attentively, and allowed me to warm to my subject. When I'd finished, he asked me what I wanted to do about it, and I told him plainly that I wanted him to keep his promise and help me realize the desire that had driven me to abandon my normal life and put myself under his tutelage. Still he listened, but again – as if he didn't know – he asked what exactly I wanted to do. So I said:

'You know what it is. I want to kill someone.'

'Go ahead and kill someone.'

'I don't know how until you teach me.'

'You don't need to know how to kill. If you want to kill somebody, you kill them.'

I sensed with that, that he was going to try and put me off again, and steeled myself for the fray. In a serious tone of voice, I began to repeat what I had said, asking him to help me fulfil my ambition, and make my position with him clear; if he did not, that would mean that he took me lightly, ridiculed me, and kept me only to run around after him.

He bit his lower lip in some distress and closed his eyes, then opened them again:

'All right – if you want to be a Child of the Night and do something that even they can't do . . . kill me. I'm serious . . . you can make a better job of it than the commissioner. I'm finished, as Sa'd Zaghlul said, I've had it. Kill me, and your name'll go down in history as the one who killed the Stranger.'

If I hadn't felt that he was in deadly earnest, I'd have lost my temper and got up and left there and then. As it was, I must admit that I even considered his suggestion for a moment.

I shook my head in a gesture of despair, and lapsed into an irritated silence, not knowing how to reply.

But he was smiling and he patted me on the shoulder without a trace of roughness, gently, just like when Warda touched me:

'It's all right. Don't be angry. I'll let you kill someone if that's what you want and you can get a certificate to prove you've passed the test. Here's the gun. The first person that comes over the bridge, from whichever direction – kill him.'

I jumped up, in my delight nearly knocking myself out on the bridge's iron girder, and cried out, painfully:

'Are you serious?'

'If you're sure you mean what you say, then I'm serious. I was happy with you, just as if you had been my own son because you've got nice gentlemanly manners and you're educated, and you understand what's going on. I could have tried to be like you instead, or to make my son like you, but if you want to be like me and you're not content with being a schoolboy, then that's that. It's serious now – either you kill the first passer-by or I kill you . . . and I'm no gentleman.'

13

So it was that we came out from under the bridge and crept along until we reached the wall that was an extension of the parapet. I had the Italian sub-machinegun and we both crouched down in readiness. Our eyes pierced the darkness, searching, for the moon had not yet risen, and in tones that were quite new to me, the Stranger whispered:

'When you see him coming, forget about yourself altogether and just concentrate on him. Don't take aim until he gets close to you – about level with that tree. When you aim, hold your breath and centre on the middle of his chest, then fire straight away.

Don't hesitate, otherwise he'll kill you. You must reckon on him being armed, and assume that if you don't get him, he'll get you. Kill or be killed. If you lose your nerve, imagine that you've got a score to settle with him. Imagine that he's the man that killed your father – even though your father's not really dead. Make yourself believe it absolutely. If he doesn't go down the first time, fire again straight away, and again. And even if he does go down, take aim and fire again. Shoot to kill.'

For the first time in my life I found myself wholly receptive to what I was being taught, listening to every word, my fingers understanding, even my breath conscious of what it would be called upon to do. I was overwhelmed by the enormity of what was about to happen, but at the same time elated, intoxicated, by what was actually happening: at long last I was learning their secrets, learning them because I'd made the grade – for if the Stranger had not had confidence in me and my abilities he would never have agreed to me becoming his pupil like this.

He was crouching beside me now and his voice and the movements of his body were beginning to take on features of his other self – the Stranger when he was preparing to attack, the Stranger as killer. But what caught my eye, and made me break out in a cold sweat which trickled uncomfortably down the middle of my back, what turned my elation into fear, was his hand closing over the axe and concealing it under his clothes. The axe which had split Shalabi's skull was waiting for me if I failed.

I felt suddenly that I'd been living with my dreams all this time, in another world, and that now the time was ripe, the moment had arrived, to bring my body to the land of my dreams; but to dream is one thing and to make our physical selves a part of our dreams quite another – and what if life itself depends on it?

He said: 'Have this.'

It was a roll-up and I had always refused to smoke in front of him, but I took it with a steady hand, and lit it, and we began to smoke like men together, and I forced myself to think of us as men together. Then he said: 'When it's all over . . . we get out of here.'

He was silent for a moment and turned to face me with a gleam in his eye: 'Perhaps we'll be lucky and land a rich one. In any case, when you've done the job make sure you've got the gun with you. Search him, take anything you find and get moving. And take care not to drop anything yourself while you're searching him.'

And I nodded my head, trying to look reassuring.

The time crawled by and we searched the distance, straining our eyes for a glimpse of our unknown victim. As the waiting grew longer, my tension increased with every minute that passed, till I could no longer bear it, and was about to stand up, shout, give vent to my pent-up emotions. But I felt his small hand reach out for my arm and press it, and he said:

'Patience. Just wait. I told you to forget about your own feelings completely. When they were teaching you to ride a bike what did they tell you? Didn't they say keep your eyes on the road, look ahead? So make sure you don't look inside yourself now or you'll be lost. Just concentrate on whoever's coming.'

His words worked like a charm, the pressure lifted, I grew calm and began to look in front of me once more.

The moon rose and at first its light was like the sunrise but then it cast a whiter light as it climbed gradually in the sky, round but not full, until it almost reached the middle and hung there like a spotlight in the roof of the world. Now that the night's sun had risen and total darkness had given way to the incomplete light of its daytime we could see the road leading up to the bridge and away from it, and the nearby fields and distant trees bathed in the half-light. We continued to watch our surroundings, noticing every change, and were rewarded for our long vigil by the flicker of a movement in the midst of this all-embracing silence.

My heart started to beat audibly, a series of rapid thuds which died away to nothing, followed immediately by another sound, far away and faint, but unmistakable – someone was singing. And my heart thudded fiercely again.

I seemed to wait a whole year until, on the horizon of the moon's daylight, the owner of the voice came into sight. At first he appeared as a white motionless spot, then moving, then as a creature whose upper half was white and its lower half black; then it became clear that he was a man mounted on an animal, and singing.

I waited for the Stranger to say something, but he made no response to my silent plea for help, even when I turned towards him. I wondered if he had seen and heard nothing, but his eyes were fastened to the moving target as if by a thread, and he never relaxed his grip on the axe.

I turned back to look at the man through the salt sweat that ran down my forehead and stung my eyes. I wiped the sweat away and got the man lined up in my sights although I didn't intend to begin taking precise aim, at the middle of his chest, until he came up parallel with the tree.

So I followed the movement of his mount unhurriedly with the muzzle of the gun, and in spite of myself began listening to the folk song which he was singing. His voice wasn't beautiful, or suited to the song he sang, but it was loud and strong; he sang 'O night', as if he were putting himself at the mercy of the night and begging it to protect him from its ills, and when he sang 'O eyes', I imagined him weeping, sorrowing for himself because the night had not heeded him. The song spoke of his lover's garden and the apricots and pomegranates and narcissi that grew there, and of how he was going to enter it and pluck its fruits. I began to be able to discern something between him and his beast – a sack that must have been full of flour – and I guessed he was late coming back from the mill.

Through all this, the Stranger remained unbelievably, inhumanly silent, a silence so profound and convincing that it could only have been designed to make me feel that he wasn't there with me at all. I was alone, the unknown man before me and the gun in my hand, with only the night to keep us company. And in spite of myself I felt as if a heavy weight had fallen from me with the realization that I was free to behave as I chose, unhindered by the presence of the Stranger and his axe. I was not afraid, not coerced, and every time I stole a glance at the Stranger and found him silent as the grave, I became more sure that I was acting independently. I was master of the situation, and I was armed and had night and the element of surprise on my side. For the first time I threw off the guise and the mentality of a disciple and felt that I was a true Son of the Night with the power to act.

Riding this wave of confidence, I began to look towards my target. Between him and the appointed tree there were now only a few yards. His voice carried clearly, lucid, the words and meanings of his song ordered and cogent. Perhaps the song, begun in fear, had done its work and made him feel at peace with the world, for it had become filled with ecstasy, as if he sang for the song itself: he sang 'O night' in praise of night's black majesty, and 'O eyes', lamenting for those that slept and deprived themselves of its beauty.

In less than a minute I had to kill this man intoxicated with his singing and his song. The muzzle of the gun followed his progress and when he was exactly level with the tree, I would take aim and shoot.

I say that I had to 'kill' him, and it was indeed no more than a word to me by that time. No aura hung around it any longer, nor any sense of revulsion: it had become a purely practical exercise, requiring me only to hold my breath, take aim, and, with a slight movement of the index finger of my right hand, pull the trigger.

The man had come much nearer and there was only about a yard between him and the tree.

I held my breath and tried to make believe that my hand was weighted with all the lead shot in the world in an effort to stop its slight trembling and to keep his chest dead in line with the sights. I pictured to myself that my father had been killed that very night and that this man was his killer coming from the scene of the crime. One movement on the trigger and it would all be over. I would enter the Kingdom of Night by its most dreaded gate. One movement, a tiny pressure.

After that I can't say exactly what happened. All I can remember is the moonlight, and the man's white gallabiyya, dazzlingly white. And his song which seemed so beautiful that it almost made the birds in the trees stop to listen. And his sense of being at peace with himself and the world, which stayed with him even when he was level with the tree and began to go past it. Everything might have been different, the course of my life itself changed, if he had been afraid, if he had stopped singing and sensed the danger; or perhaps if I had believed more effectively that he had killed my father; or something had happened outside the control of either of us, something to scratch at the wall of inviolability surrounding him and moving with him, neutralizing any evil directed at him. For to this day I don't know why my finger didn't perform that insignificant movement and squeeze the trigger. How could I explain the voice welling up from the depths of me, from the tips of my toes, the roots of my hair, my guts? I'd never heard it before, never contemplated its existence nor taken account of it, never thought that at the last minute, something inside me would say, 'Thou shalt not'.

All the time, so unthinkingly, we put prohibitions on others and they accept or refuse them, unthinkingly too. But to enforce it on myself, and at a moment like that, threw me into disarray, and the thought of it still perplexes me.

I sweated copiously from every part of my body: little seas came into being in the palm of my hand and on the ball of the very finger that was meant to play such a decisive part in the whole business. The gun almost fell from my grasp and my finger slipped on the trigger every time it tried to squeeze it. My sweat was no doubt also the reason for the flaccidity of my will which I tried to summon into action against the voice inside me, cursing it, questioning its source, disgusted that it should apparently dissolve all my will-power and paralyze every part of me down to my last finger-joint.

Eventually I recognized its source: the man, singing at the top of his voice now, lord of all he surveyed. He had no presentiment of evil evidently, and at the sight of him in his turban and white gallabiyya, with his sack of flour, I felt the distance between us evaporating. I had come to know the words of his song, seen a meaning in them, and it seemed to me that he was singing to me, greeting me perhaps. His stick on the animal's back, the rhythmic jogging of his legs against its flanks, each reverberation of his throat as he sang, came to me in the form of an imperious command: 'Thou shalt not.' In the end everything he did which characterized him as a human being evoked this reaction in me, even the way – peculiar to mankind – in which he sat upright astride his mount. These responses in me accumulated to form an impenetrable defence around him and he moved as if in a wide sacred circle which inevitably reached out to touch me, and immobilized me. I was affected by it to the extent that when he was within a hairsbreadth of the bridge and caught sight of us and passed the time of day, I felt the gun slipping out of my grasp, and heard myself replying: 'Greetings and the peace of God . . .'

When he was parallel with us, he excused himself for passing us without dismounting. A voice replied from down beside me – I had forgotten all about him: 'You're welcome. Please don't worry.'

I began to remember in more precise detail the fate which awaited me. Strangely enough I was without fear, and with complete indifference I was ready to die, even to stand up to the Stranger if he tried to make good my failure.

14

But he didn't kill me, nor did he try to kill the man. And I began to talk, trying to explain, but he laid a hand on my shoulder and said: 'There's no need for that . . . this axe was ready for you it's true . . .' I asked him why then he hadn't used it. To my surprise he said that he would have done only if I'd shot the man and killed him. This astonished me and made me listen, although he didn't say much. Being up to his ears in crime and killing, he couldn't have let me go the same way even if I'd wanted to. If I'd done it once, there would have been no looking back, and I would have become like him and lived the miserable life that he lived, compelled, in self-preservation, to destroy the lives of others. Tormented, and tormenting others, hating them to the death and being hated by them in turn, in the end I'd turn traitor like Shalabi: if I dealt honourably with people, I'd pay for it with my life, and if I didn't doubt everybody I came across, however sincere they seemed, I'd be lost . . .

'It's a terrible life when you don't trust anybody and nobody trusts you and you don't believe what anybody tells you and they don't believe you . . . You're better off dead. And the tragedy is that you can't kill yourself – you can kill as many people as you want and still you won't be able to kill yourself. That's why I would have taken pity on you and killed you. I only wish I could meet somebody who'd have the guts to do the same for me.'

He was silent for a moment, staring at the moon, then, as if talking to himself, he said:

'At least if you had killed him, I would have known that it was no use trusting you any more. Once a man's killed somebody, he's like a she-wolf ready to eat her cubs, a mad dog whose sole occupation is to turn on people indiscriminately, even his friends and companions. At the very least you would have informed on me.'

He fell silent again and took the gun from me and began to

examine it. Then he went on:

'I've got to wake up, it's obvious. I'll get you into the same hole that I'm in. I've put you through a lot. All this time I've been hoping that I'd close my eyes one day and wake up to find that I was your father, and that you were my son. But it's clear that your real father has priority over me. Now – move.'

I was bewildered, wrapped up in what he was saying, and his last words took me by surprise. His tone was changed utterly, his voice decisive and clipped, with not a trace of hesitation or compassion in it. I stared at him with wide astonished eyes, and he stared back unmoved, hard, cold and stern: 'Get going. And don't stop running till you're home.'

A terrible explosion rang out, and a burst of hot compressed air passed just above my shoulder, nearly taking my ear off. When I came to my senses I was running, and another explosion sounded far off, and above my head a hail of bullets blazed and spat, puncturing the air. But I, although I never stopped running, dared to glance backwards once at the Stranger, knowing that it would be for the last time. Perhaps it was an optical illusion, but it seemed to me that I was still and he was running. He looked very old, his shoulders weighed down by their burden, his short figure plunging into the night, swallowed up in its depths, merging with the blackness which retreated before the searchlights of dawn.

The Black Policeman
⊂⊃⊂⊃⊂⊃⊂⊃
1

When I say there was something about Shawqi which disturbed
me, and I didn't know what caused it, or how to account for it, I
don't mean many of the more obvious manifestations of it. There
was the famous smile that didn't express anything, but was like a
mask put on when he wanted to hide from people, or the opa-
queness in his eyes that was there to deflect your gaze and prevent
your eyes meeting his even for a second – as if in that second you
would grasp his mystery and understand what was wrong with
him. There was his strange behaviour in social gatherings when
he would astonish people with his sudden outbursts of emotion at
a word let slip by one of those present; and then a few seconds
later, he would be on his feet and out of the door, having
fabricated some excuse, with no hint of concern for his credibility
in the eyes of the gathering.

What I mean is something that I cannot express precisely,
could not even discover when I was forced to be an eyewitness to a
horrifying encounter whose minutest details I still trace in my
mind's eye when I am sitting alone, in the hope that perhaps I
may see the weak, trembling thing that Shawqi clasps firmly to
himself. And I would claim that very occasionally I have almost
managed to pin it down, no more than that; to be honest with
myself I realize that as I sit here to write what happened I have
only one aim: to succeed by means of writing where I have failed
in my silent reflections. I'm taking a gamble, and who knows,
when I finish I may have explained everything and reached the
truth; so far my efforts in this direction have just left me confused.

2

Our starting-point is unremarkable. I could never have imagined
that it would lead me to any mystery, important or otherwise. It

is the chief medical officer's room in the old county hall, demolished long ago now. Every time I found myself in Bab al-Khalq Square with its famous clock, the façade of the national library, and the minaret rising up from the square like a high waterless fountain, I remembered Shawqi, and felt driven instinctively to go and look him up. He was working in the regional medical office and had chosen to be on duty in the afternoon, perhaps because at this time of day he could be his own boss. The chief medical officer only worked in the mornings, and being in charge of the office, sitting in the boss's chair, acknowledging the greetings of the office employees and those who came on business there, were pleasures that could not fail to gratify the pride of any young doctor, while in the mornings he was merely a subordinate, one of four or five others. We were sitting there in that office when the orderly Abdullah addressed him.

'This one's not worth bothering with, sir. He makes noises, barks like dogs, howls like wolves.'

At first I assumed it to be one of the exaggerations for which the orderly was well known in the office, especially when it came to reckoning up the prices of tea and coffee and sandwiches. He had come there from the army medical corps as office messenger but they had found him quicker on his feet and more intelligent than the existing medical orderly and given him the job. The apparently submissive way in which he addressed the doctors, his broad gleaming forehead obsequiously inclined, gave these civilians a taste of the pleasurable sense of power enjoyed by military men. His accustomed stance before the half-open door of the chief medical officer's room as he scolded late-comers and invented stories to get rid of them had become one of the main distractions of my meetings with Shawqi.

Had it not been for the ring of truth in what he said neither of us would have taken any notice of him, and I had become used to drifting off into my own thoughts if Shawqi was taken up with talking to Abdullah about work. But this jerked me out of my daydreaming and made me ask who it was that howled and barked, to learn that he was the subject of a huge dossier on Shawqi's desk.

It was almost half-past four, in summertime, and the room had emptied of its callers. Most of those who came were the very poor, beggars and tramps, some mad or physically deformed, people pressing false charges, and coming to have their claims verified by the experts, or simply people coming to be treated for injuries sustained in their disputes. They came singly and in groups, some in chains and handcuffs, or tied up with their own clothes to prevent them escaping from the policemen guarding them.

Witth them were their official reports and notes from police stations requiring medical examinations to assess their ages and the nature of their infirmities, preliminaries to the long chain of processing they were to undergo. There would always be the occasional better-dressed person or a girl from a good family involved in some scandal, an accusation of rape perhaps, and, inevitably, there were the military and police personnel, including officers, applying for medical certificates. There had been a huge crowd starting at the main door of the building, filling its vast courtyard, and ending in the outstretched arms of Abdullah who was blocking the open doorway of the medical office begging them hoarsely, and in vain, to wait their turn. The miracle was that Shawqi finished with them all in no more than an hour, but what an hour it was! And even when the room was empty and Abdullah had fastened the door behind them, the air remained full of ghosts who almost seemed to come between us and interrupt our conversation.

Ghosts of them and their miseries lingered behind, and the traces of their distinctive smells, not offensive, as might be supposed, but different certainly from the smell of professional men, or peasants. They only became offensive when they mingled with the smell of the carbolic acid used to clean the floors, and DDT, and the sweat of the ancient building and its broken-down furniture. On a summer's afternoon like that one all these clung together, transformed into a steamy closeness that hung in the air, filling the room to its high ceiling; we would be stifled by it, almost driven to leave the place, but we stayed because, perversely, these feelings of external suffocation afforded us considerable relief from our feelings of suffocation within.

Both Shawqi and I belonged to what was known by common consent as 'the confused generation', but there was no particular reason for us to be friends. The Seccnd World War had contrived for us to be in the same faculty of the university together, with nothing in common as far as our political affiliations and opinions about people and life in general were concerned. The fact that we were friends did not indicate a frivolous attitude in either of us towards our differences, and conceivably we were too serious, each of us prepared almost to kill to defend his own position. Perhaps the reason for our great friendship, and the basis for my continuing relationship with Shawqi, was that we had a common mission in life. Although we envisaged the means differently, we both believed that we were destined to save our country and change the fate of our people radically and for ever.

We first met in the student's conference that we organized in the faculty, and almost came to blows there, although we drank tea together afterwards and he confided to me that he had agreed with what I had been saying but that in the situation he had been obliged to defend the other members of his group. That point may have been settled, but we found in the days that followed that the opinions and beliefs of each of us were abhorrent to the other, and so it was strange that at the same time we grew closer.

Ours may have been one generation but it was split into factions with very different preoccupations. Some of our contemporaries had all-night poker sessions playing for pennies, saying they were gambling, others skipped lectures constantly and went in groups to the cinema matinees. There were those whose main interest in life was sport, running around playing-fields in their vests, and there were the terrorist groups, the hit men; while we remained totally absorbed in organizing conferences, making speeches – the business of politics. We exchanged insults with the athletes and the capricious, calling them emasculated when they called us fanatical, and amongst ourselves the labels of fascist and communist, bigot and heretic flew back and forth; but we were all encompassed by the wide arc of politics, the subject which we held in common veneration.

Shawqi himself had always irritated me before I knew him: when he got up to speak there was something of the charlatan in his manner, a man with a cheap and dubious commodity to sell in the market-place. Even his physical appearance had not attracted me: his face was strangely pale which intensified the blackness of his thick moustache, and I had never come to terms with this moustache in the first place, unable to define exactly how it was out of keeping with his chin as it grew luxuriantly while his chin was smooth and free of stubble, like an adolescent's. He was thin, of average height, with an expression so serious that it could not help but engender attitudes of frivolity or doubt.

Still, he was one of the leaders in the faculty and of his political group, and welcomed controversy with a self-assured smile, never losing his temper. His greatest fault, which I was often to regret, was that he was in the other camp, and I used to dream that one day I would be able to convince him that we could ultimately agree. But these were just dreams, for Shawqi rejoiced in a tremendous strength of will, and it was as if he had been born knowing exactly what he wanted and certain that he would achieve it. As a result his belief seemed to grow daily more profound and tenacious, so that it was inconceivable that a new belief could ever shake it.

But then came the political event which rocked the whole country, and Shawqi was arrested and put in prison to await trial. And perhaps because I believed in him so much and respected him as one of the leaders of our generation, I was surprised at how little regret there was at his disappearance from the faculty, even among the few remaining members of his group. Every time I asked about him I received a vague reply and there was an evasion of any real answers as to the fate of Shawqi and all the others of differing political persuasions arrested at the same time.

This was the first serious blow dealt to our generation. We had emerged from the Second World War to find armies of occupation carousing in our lands. We rose up and they insulted us with a formal withdrawal to the Canal Zone. We rose up again demanding total withdrawal and armed resistance to the occupation, and this time they pounded us. A certain Right Honourable Gentleman ordered the massacre on the Abbas Bridge – when we were marching from the university to the city centre and the authorities opened the bridge so that hundreds of us fell in and were killed or wounded. He tried to hit us still harder, but he was assassinated, so they brought in another one to complete the job. The prisons were opened wide, and the reign of terror began: mouths were closed, voices suppressed, informers were let loose in the universities. Now where there had been meetings and political discussions there was a war of nerves with its attendant rumours and prevailing sense of fear, and our faculty seethed with secret police. A whole generation was scattered, some to prison, some into exile in the countryside or in far-off towns and cities, and some inside themselves, digging great holes there where they buried their rebellion and their beliefs and covered them over, a little more each day, as they pretended what they did not think.

It was at this time that rumours of torture spread and the Black Policeman became notorious, and stories were told of what he did to prisoners and detainees. He became a symbol for us of the beatings that we had received and his name evoked fear; now, after all these years, his file was lying on Shawqi's desk.

3

This has not been an attempt at historical documentation, merely a glance at events before we return to Shawqi, for many months went by after contact between us had been abruptly broken off, and I did not see him again until the day of the final examination. I was taken quite by surprise when he came into the examination hall with a group of his fellow-prisoners, in handcuffs, surrounded by policemen and armed guards. Over the examiners and the question papers we exchanged smiles, taking care not to do it openly, as if unseen eyes would notice our action and it would be recorded. For haven't I said already that we were living in a reign of terror and surely such a reign's principal achievement is to succeed in making each of us responsible for terrorizing himself, keeping his own mouth shut and submitting to the existing state of affairs.

When the results came out I learnt, again to my surprise, that Shawqi had passed. How he could have studied a subject which normally depends on so much practical work and experience, and answered the questions at all, let alone well enough to pass, I can't say, but he did it, and still he was not released or sent for trial, or even charged — things which only happen in ages of darkness, or in a country which, despite the enlightened state of the world in general, is still living in the dark ages.

A long time went by before his release and I knew nothing of it until I happened to be walking through the department of the big hospital where I worked after my graduation, and noticed him sitting in the doctor's room looking hesitant and embarrassed as if he had come to visit a patient. Then I discovered that he had been appointed to the same unit as myself, and even as I was taken up in the clamour of greeting, I couldn't help noticing how he had changed. For a second I thought it wasn't he for there were manifest physical differences: he had become flabby as prisoners do and, an unprecedented development, his beard had sprouted and grown, making him look altogether darker. Nevertheless, I gave him a hero's welcome, and as such I continued to treat him. I was not alone in this: the other doctors and nurses in the unit and some of the patients who were familiar with the story of the new doctor all treated him as a returning hero and expected him to play the part. We accepted his behaviour at first as symptomatic of some kind of modesty and desire for self-effacement.

My graduation had had its effect on my view of people and things and taken the edge off my confidence in my beliefs and opinions. I began to give credence to goodness and courage wherever they existed, and to welcome every sincere act even if it orginated with those who did not share my opinions and were hostile to my beliefs. And so my dearest wish was that an appropriate occasion would arise when I could sit down with Shawqi and he would tell me everything that had happened to him, all the significant incidents and moments of heroism that there surely must have been. In fact there were numerous occasions, but my questions never found answers, and worse than that, Shawqi seemed to be in some kind of state where I sensed that he had a fundamental aversion to questions. At first I had thought it was some kind of excessive caution on his part, whereby he wanted to avoid talking in front of the patients or in the hearing of the other staff, that at the very worst he was postponing the conversation to some time in the not-too-distant future.

But the days went by and he clung firmly to his position, a problem which at first I did not take too seriously, never dreaming that it would lead me to any sort of discovery, although I did begin subconsciously to observe Shawqi more closely. At no time did I intend to do more than extricate him from what I thought was a temporary and very natural condition that had affected him as a result of coming out of prison, to bring back the Shawqi I had known. Despite the fact that we had been poles apart, I was convinced that he was not the type of person to abandon his views after a few months in prison; even though, at that time, we used to come across so many of our acquaintances and friends who had been full of enthusiasm before their imprisonment but who came out having severed every link with politics and the nationalist movement, as if prison were the excuse they had been waiting for to retreat from the battle.

As I was saying, I began to pay more attention to Shawqi, and what I noticed first was that his eyes bore a mark, an imprint of something that had not been there before. Before, there had always been a light in his eye, and his face had acquired a particular attraction from the deep conviction which glowed through his being and expressed itself on his face, concentrated in his eyes, conveying to the world an image of his spirit. That light had died, and all that was left was a dull glimmer, a mere indication that life was present. It unnerved me to look into his eyes, but I never discovered the reason until long afterwards.

I began to notice that his voice had changed, and he only talked in a whisper, the polite subdued mumblings of one who always expects his requests to be turned down. He moved through his life like a blinkered beast, looking only at what was right under his nose. And this was the man who had always looked about him, exploring, seeing beneath the surface, the man who flared up in anger when his eye fell upon an injustice, warning the world of the consequences of its evil-doing and threatening it with change.

Gradually, during the two or three months that we worked together, I was no longer able to avoid being affected by the strange state of isolation which Shawqi preserved, and I almost gave up hope that he would one day emerge from his cocoon of silence and tell me what had happened to him behind bars. I began to believe, inevitably, that he had not only changed, but was a different person altogether. Many times I would catch him making petty deals, so that, for example, he would be given the hernia operations to do more often than me or his other colleagues. Frequently, I would hear him currying favour with the consultant, who was only a year ahead of us in age and seniority, getting him to lend him books or let him be at his elbow during the examination of a patient. And he lied, lied continually and without reason, in such a naive way, easily discovered and arousing only scorn. I didn't believe the rumours which the staff nurse spread about him until I saw with my own eyes how he would attend patients in the cubicle where the dressings were changed and made despicable cheap bargains with them, undertaking to take special care of them, and accepting in exchange a few coins, all that a sick man lying in a government hospital would possess.

We also noticed, living in the hostel with him, that every time he went into one of our rooms, something would disappear, even if it was only an old toothbrush, so much so that there used to be a saying: 'If Shawqi shakes your right hand, keep hold of your wallet with your left.' The doctors who had recently graduated used to discuss Shawqi, and agreed that he was sick, a kleptomaniac; it was hard for me to watch them talking about him and acknowledge that Shawqi, whom they had always considered as a leader when they were students, had become not only a butt for their jokes, but an object of scorn and derision as well. Out of a hundred or so doctors he, their erstwhile leader, was the one whom they all despised.

I have no desire to enumerate all the irregularities of his behaviour during that year of our specialization, or afterwards – the clinics that he procured for himself, the cheating, the embezzling, the strange venomous glances he cast at patients, and at people in general; the way he cut himself off from his family after he graduated and refused to give them so much as a penny; how he came to get married, the devious way too that he obtained his diploma and engineered his being appointed in this office. Nor will I go into his inhumane handling of callers to the office, especially police personnel applying for medical certificates. I once saw a policeman crying in front of him, imploring him not to let the authorities know that he was only pretending to be ill, for fear that he would be brought to trial and lose his pay; and the entreaties, the humiliation, the tears only made Shawqi smile, his face contorted with cruel pleasure, the more remarkable for being at least as real as the man's tears.

Why, in view of all this, I kept up with Shawqi, I find it difficult to explain, for I suffered from his offensive behaviour at least as much as the others. But I couldn't just write him off as a kleptomaniac, or even simply as someone who had undergone a personality change as the result of a spell in prison. I refused to believe that a few months in prison could drive a human being from one extreme to another, and I found it inconceivable that all that remained of the old Shawqi was a dazzling smile that he was proficient in using to his best advantage: despite the element of exaggeration in it, this smile always appeared enervated, and never extended beyond his lips. With it he passed the time of day with his private patients, said good morning to his wife, returned the orderly's greeting, and masked his features when discomfited by a question of mine. It was a smile that faithfully epitomized success, in the loosely-defined superficial meaning of the word.

I saw things from a different perspective: I continued to believe that Shawqi was not a lost cause, that his behaviour was not more than the purely temporary reflections of the layers of pain which encrusted his personality, and that it would pass. Its passing, moreover, depended on me, and his survival was in my hands. I could leave him to sink without trace or else I could preserve our relationship, trying always to help him retrieve what he once had been, never giving in to despair.

His present state convinced me that something grave and dreadful had happened. I looked at him and observed minute details of his behaviour, and had the impression that he had been wounded, not locally or specifically, but in some fundamental all-embracing fashion. Instead of Shawqi, I was looking at a huge scar which the wound had left behind. And the more I looked, the more stubbornly I came to believe that every wrong in him could be put right, every wound healed; and my optimism was not born out of my own private hope. Somewhere in Shawqi, under many layers, there was an area of him, the nature and scope of which I could not quite ascertain; all I can say is that it was perhaps a part of him that felt an overwhelming desire to hear somebody talk, whose only outlet was me, and then only on those occasions, few and far between, when I met him, sometimes when he had a clinic, sometimes in his office. There we would sit for hours exchanging the most trifling conversation about what mutual acquaintances were doing now and about the doctor's new salary scale.

There was always at least one occasion in the course of these encounters when Shawqi would suddenly turn aside, as if he wanted to hide his emotion from me. He would ask me questions about the situation in a way which made me aware of the hunger inside him, a craving that was gnawing at his insides. And when I answered, I never came up with anything new, just talked in the manner which we who are interested in politics, of whatever persuasion, know how to do so well.

Shawqi always refused to express opinions and indeed when I talked he consciously acted as if the subject of the conversation were wholly irrelevant to him, or as if he had no connection, direct or indirect, with anything outside himself and his immediate concerns. But still I could always tell that, despite the façade, he was listening, with a longing and a delight that he usually succeeded in hiding. If I fell silent he roused me with some unimportant question or interrupted the silence by inhaling on another cigarette, taking in the smoke as if he wanted to quench a burning thirst with it. This was the man who, when we were students, had always lectured me on the harmful effects of smoking and the undesirable moral implications of it. Now the nails and upper-finger joints of both hands were stained brown with tobacco.

So we would sit on, as I revealed my inner thoughts volubly, he with extreme caution. Many times I found myself carefully observing the scene, in a neutral detached frame of mind, and then I could see us, two individuals from our confused generation that had taken its mission so gravely upon itself as to be almost crushed by the weight of it. We sat in a locked examination room or in the office with its laden air, smoking excessively as if bent on self-destruction, and even as we filled the place with a dense cloud from our cigarettes and our hearts burning, this did not stop us from lighting more cigarettes and allowing our passions to rage still more furiously, as if the increasing pressure from the outside would somehow expel from our hearts what weighed so heavily there: the leaden misery left behind in us, dragging our spirits downwards, making us prematurely bowed. The fates, it seemed, had conspired to isolate us from our generation, just as they had divided it against itself, and had trapped us within these interlocking bottlenecks of walls and smoke and our fears.

Between us two there was a constant chase which never reached a conclusion. I, a drowning man, was trying to catch hold of Shawqi and pull him to the surface and he, terrified, refused, but I persisted as if all I had fought for and believed in was crystallized in my attempts to save him. He, on the other hand, seemed dedicated to drowning still deeper, taking me with him if he could, and oh the mockery of it, when in the past we had worked in the certain hope that we would save our whole people, and now each of us was powerless even to save himself.

For hours we would sit like this, never noticing the time except when some external factor drew our attention to it – night falling, a telephone ringing insistently, or an occurrence that was out of the ordinary, like Abdullah's comment on the file which, had I known it, was to lead Shawqi and me towards the fateful events of that summer's afternoon.

4

Abdullah didn't say to begin with that it was the Black Policeman. All he said in reply to Shawqi's question was:

'He's a difficult one, sir, and he can't get any worse. We don't need to bother about him. We can leave him to the boss when he comes in the morning; he'll know what to do with him.'

At the time Shawqi was engaged in one of his routine operations which consisted of going through the notes of messages telephoned into the office requiring medical certificates for sick military and police personnel. He did this with his own best interests at heart, since he sifted out any one which referred to an address near his clinic if he wanted to go there, or near his home. In this way he could save himself the trouble of going by bus or tram or in his own car, as he would surreptitiously get the office's station wagon to take him on where he wanted to go when he had finished his official duties.

In the course of this exercise he had stumbled upon the file, and Abdullah had volunteered his information about the patient in question. The advice which he had subsequently proffered on the subject was, like most of Abdullah's advice, more in the nature of an incontrovertible order. Although he was only the office orderly, barely able to read and write, he had become more or less the sole custodian of the rules and regulations of the medical department all the time he worked there, and consequently if difficulties arose he was the ultimate source of reference in solving them. His opinion was binding as, however much the chief medical officer and the other doctors objected, it was always established finally that his was the correct one and the one which conformed to everything laid down by the rules and regulations. Shawqi in particular never argued with him as the thing he feared most of all was that by some misfortune he should one day err in his interpretation of some rule or regulation of the place – he, who had started out as the enemy of every established principle. Now responsibility was his own arch-enemy and he would do anything to avoid it, going to ridiculous lengths to escape one clause which seemed to enjoin an iota of responsibility upon him. Sometimes it seemed to me that he would have liked best to fade away into some kind of ethereal state of being in which he would not have had even the responsibility of finding for himself a space to occupy on the surface of the earth, nor to have borne the burden of being looked at by his fellow men. At the same time he clung to life and the things of the world with such astonishing appetite that it seemed he would have swallowed them up inside him if he could have done.

I took the opportunity of the exchange between Shawqi and Abdullah to reach out for the file. I had always been consumed with curiosity about such files for I had often seen them in government departments stamped with the words 'Highly Confidential', but had been prevented from looking through them by the rule which said that only heads of departments could look at them, and then only in extreme cases. This one had more than a hundred sheets in it, the first of which was a birth certificate. I found it an amusing coincidence that Abbas Mahmud al-Zanfali, subject of the file and owner of the birth certificate, was born in the same year as me, and a few months before Shawqi. I had pictured that he would be old, or at least in his forties, only to discover to my surprise that he was one of us.

I went on turning the pages. The file was more like a book, the life of a man. A life which had clearly been disturbed from the beginning, restless, never staying on a straight path. The first half of his service was a record of penalties he had incurred and adverse reports on his behaviour, despite the attached statement from two government employees testifying to his good conduct. There were other sections, mostly dealing with his many different postings and assignments. Then there was a letter crowned with the cabinet letterhead saying that he was to become part of the ministerial bodyguard. From that page onwards there was no record of cautions or deductions from his wages, instead a sudden deluge of wage increases, then an order that he should be promoted to the rank of corporal, then another stating that, because his was an exceptional case, he was to be promoted to sergeant. After that there was a copy of a letter of thanks and appreciation from the minister of the interior, then the copy of a decision to award him a duty medal, second-class, 'in grateful recognition of his untiring efforts in the execution of his duty and of his self-sacrifice in the service of the highest interests of the nation'.

But all this did not take up more than a small part of the file, and most of the pages were requests for sick leave and letters exchanged between the chief constable's office and the interior ministry and the regional health board. The first of these was written on a day in November 1949 and the last years later, or to be precise on the previous day. It was the reply to a letter which the administration had sent to Shawqi's boss asking him to carry out a medical examination on the said Abbas Mahmud al-Zanfali to establish his total incapacity, as a prelude to dismissing him from the service.

As I was looking at the last page I picked up the tail-end of the conversation between Shawqi and the orderly. The latter was saying confidentially, 'Don't you know who Abbas Mahmud al-Zanfali is, sir?' And before Shawqi could begin to reply, he went on: 'He's the one they used to call the Black Policeman, sir. Don't tell me you've never heard of him.'

Shawqi did not reply. He merely stiffened slightly and his expression did not change. He said nothing, and showed no signs of astonishment or horror. After a moment or two he took the file from me and began to flick through its pages, but still neither his face nor his body betrayed the slightest tremor of emotion, and he said not a word. How much time went by while Shawqi sat there reading, I couldn't begin to judge, as my attention was completely taken up with his own compulsive involvement in what he was doing. Such was the intensity of his concentration that it wasn't apparent from his expression, but you could feel it, almost touch it, and it seemed that every part of his body was on the alert as he crouched over the pages.

In all the years we had known each other it was the first time I had ever seen him wholly absorbed in one thing. For usually, like rays passing through a concave lens, his senses never fell on one thing at a time or focused on a single point. He was continually diverging, his energies concentrated in different directions at once as if there was an evenly charged tension between the parts preventing them from coming together; his dealings with himself and with people and things outside him had never seemed to bear any relation to time and space.

5

I savoured the situation with childlike relish as I sat in the back seat of the official car next to Shawqi. The driver exploited his official immunity to break whatever rules he pleased and drove at a reckless speed ignoring the insults hurled at him by pedestrians and fellow motorists, or replying to them with worse ones of his own, *sotto voce*, showing a due regard for propriety. Beside him sat Abdullah, never pausing for breath, repeating insistently that we should leave the matter for the boss's attention the next day. His discomfiture at the duty which had fallen to him was plain to see; a medical examination on an old colleague to certify him as unfit and throw him out of a job was something that made him uneasy and he was refusing to be present at it or have any part in it.

The only one of us who was completely silent was Shawqi. He no longer smiled his empty smile and his mind was obviously in turmoil as we drove to our destination. He seemed convulsed with silent pain, crying out inside where I had thought him shrivelled up like the core of a withered palm tree.

My childish pleasure was not wholly unjustified, for despite all that the newspapers had written about the Black Policeman I had scarcely entertained the possibility that he really existed. Even when Abduallah had assured us that this Abbas was the Black Policeman I had suspended my belief in his existence until I could see him with my own eyes. For this reason, not only was I happy to accompany Shawqi, but I had actually asked him if I might. It was not the first time that I had gone on his rounds with him, but the only time that I had invited myself, from an absolute sense of an opportunity not to be missed rather than mere curiosity, a chance to see the man who was such a symbolic figure for our generation, a part of it as much as the terrors of the prisons and the glories of the armed struggle.

Once again I tried to ask Shawqi about him, certain that from his time in prison he must know the reality that lay behind his becoming so important for us. I had tried so often and failed, and been surprised how, every time he had sensed the question dancing on the tip of my tongue or forming itself into words, his eyes had taken on their veiled look, allowing him to appear preoccupied by something more important, a patient he was treating, or whatever it may have been. It seemed that in this way he pretended, not only to me, but even to himself, that he had not so much as heard the question. And even on this occasion he ignored it and took refuge in the strange operations of his own mind. But I didn't give up. I repeated the question insistently, modifying it all the time, lowering my sights to the point where all that I wanted to know was whether Shawqi, during all the time he was in prison, had ever caught sight of the policeman. I was relieved, of course, and not a little surprised, but my main feeling was one of some dread, when Shawqi finally opened his mouth and answered: 'Yes, I did.'

I felt like a lawyer when, not after a day in court, but a thousand days, a gleam of light comes to him with the stray word of a witness, and the ghost of a confession begins to haunt him. Immediately I asked him another question: 'You mean everything the newspapers said was true?'

After a moment's hesitation Shawqi said: 'It's possible. But the Black Policeman meant something else to us. Something else altogether. The gossip, the sex scandals, that you heard about didn't mean anything to us.'

Again my curiosity was aroused and, using all my powers of persuasion, gently yet more persistently, I went on probing. Still I did not succeed in getting more than a few words out of him and most of these were only the muttered grunts of someone disinterested in anything conveyed to him by his senses from the outside world. I was only to learn the answer to my question in the days that followed as I pondered over events, or pieced together evidence on the basis of glimpses I caught of the treatise which Shawqi was engrossed in writing and which was intended to be kept a secret from me. But I do not want to portray events in such a way as to suggest that the particular aspect which I learnt about provided a complete rationale for Shawqi's odd behaviour after he came out of prison. In this case the story would appear as simplistic and naive as the plots of commercial films or radio plays – a man goes into prison with one personality and comes out with another, and the mystery of his transformation continues to keep his friend awake at night until something happens which cuts the Gordian knot, the hero talks, the riddle is solved and the problem is no more.

If only man were like that. If only like a problem in engineering or mathematics, he submitted to one law or could be explained by a handful of theories. But instead the more we know of a person, the more difficult it becomes to understand him, and the truth which we perceive as the key to his whole mystery is in fact no more than a step on the way to areas of whose very existence we were ignorant. So we are led to more discoveries which in turn provoke us to go in pursuit of truths beyond those we have already ascertained.

The change in Shawqi could not be traced back to a specific cause, nor explained in terms of a mystery. His silence, the way he shunned political activity and refused even to talk politics, was not the result of some psychological problem that had developed in him, nor even of simple fear. What had happened to him was something different, a change more like a butterfly emerging from a chrysalis, or the transformation of wood into ashes by fire. But in this case the wood had not disintegrated and I had begun to realize, especially more recently, that I had been wrong all along and that my attempts to 'save' Shawqi were doomed to failure. I had entered upon them in the belief that Shawqi had undergone some damaging change, the effects of which it would be possible to repair. Now it seemed to me that things were completely different from how I had pictured them. The Shawqi who had entered prison had not come out again.

The man who had come out was another person with other characteristics – even my use of the word person is no more than a kind of simplification. To us he seemed an alien creature, of whom the most disturbing feature was the many resemblances he bore to the Shawqi we had known, and to the millions of other human beings crowding the earth's surface whom he joined on his release. He talked like them, got annoyed, planned ahead for the future, fell in love; and even in his fear of plunging deeply into certain subjects he was not unlike them.

The differences only came to light after much time spent in his company and prolonged scrutiny of his behaviour amounting to an abnormal interest in the subject. Then you came to realize, as I had done, that the difference between Shawqi and other people was buried deep, far below the conventional layers of behaviour, perhaps in his basic driving force. Although he appeared human in the superficial aspects of his behaviour, it no longer seemed possible to classify him with the rest of humanity, sane or insane, sick or deviant. He required separate classification, having departed from the rest in order to live in accord with an extraordinary impulse: not to procreate, grow, or even merely survive, but to run away. It was as if the whole of humanity had taken on a demoniac nature in his eyes, and was bent on destroying him. His fellow human beings, declared enemies, were lying in wait for him and would not rest until he was routed.

His tragedy was that he must continue to live alongside those whom he dreaded and feared. He was forced to have dealings with them, be involved in their affairs and have them involved in his, make friends and colleagues of them, while all the time he was eaten up by terror. His life had no structure, his will played no part in it, there was no distant goal which he strove to realize that gave him a reason for staying alive. Running away had become the purpose of his existence. His flight was not simply a renouncing of conventional responsibilities so that he could wander free and untrammelled like a mystic or a holy man: it had to take place while he continued to live among men, and became thereby a highly complicated operation, conceivably taking up a whole lifetime.

What could be more piteously strange than someone who has lost the basic sense of security which comes from being a human being among others? It was as if a rabid dog from the pack that he ran with had attacked him and, realizing that he had escaped with his skin that time, he had mobilized all his resources to avoid a second injury. Mankind to him was no more than a pack of dogs or wolves, devils from whom there was no escape; even his fancy could contrive no friendly other planet or far-off desert island where he could live in peace. They lay in wait for him everywhere: he had to meet them all the time, talk to them and acknowledge that his destiny was bound up with theirs, but never could he allow his fear to show itself.

Imagine walking through a place crawling with wild beasts, your hair on end, ears alive to the faintest sound, ready to run at any moment and at the same time feigning carelessness. So Shawqi went about his business without betraying any fear, moving quite calmly and naturally, his expressions confirming his lack of concern. Some days cheerful, others irritable, he created the illusion that he was a human being just like the rest of them, desiring to differentiate himself from them only by appearing stronger and more self-assured.

His life had no aim, no structure, he did not bring his will to bear on the course of it and had no desire to achieve any goals either long-term or short-term, since his sole purpose was to avoid the danger always lurking, and live from moment to moment. He did not construct his life by means of actions placed one on top of the other to form a pyramid, but dug downwards making a tortuous network of burrows. Whenever he sensed danger he dug deeper into another temporary refuge.

He made a friend or a colleague out of you in his efforts to escape from you, engaging you in conversation to distract attention from himself, or doing you favours and pretending to be nice to you in order to put you off the scent. He got married to escape the responsibility of being unmarried. He worked for the regional health board to escape the possibility of being an object of interest for the security services, even though that meant running straight into their arms. He had come to recognize that he was surrounded on all sides by a dangerous species; if he cried out for help, no one would come running to the rescue, on the contrary, they would all see that he had fallen and rush to eat him alive. So he was on his own, his own best friend and truest confidant. His life was a constant struggle never to disclose that he was always on the alert, to keep his violent fears and desires buried away out of sight, at the same time appearing to hide nothing. He tried to preserve an opaque impenetrable exterior while he held his own world tight inside him, concealed from the eyes of the world.

He defied definition, having nothing of the criminal mentality, not wishing harm to anybody, or harbouring grudges. His only desire was to be safe, but if he was forced to inflict pain he did it viciously, choosing his victim with care. Still he was not vengeful, nor did he wish to render evil to the evil that surrounded him. His motive was not even self-defence, the justification of many a criminal act. He caused injury merely in order to merge with his surroundings, wearing devil's clothing as a disguise, perhaps as the most effective way of hiding the truth from prying eyes. If only they had realized his overwhelming desire for life, greater than all theirs compounded, yet tempered always by his dreadful frenzied fear of every living creature.

This being that emerged from prison retaining few of his links with humankind still used his human wit and all that his life as a man had bestowed upon him: for he moved away from them and became fundamentally different, yet he expended abnormal amounts of energy and inventiveness in burying these differences deep inside him, so that he appeared more conformist than the rest, outdoing them all in his normality.

You would be justified in asking how I knew all this, and I wouldn't go so far as to say that I arrived at these perceptions entirely as a result of my own efforts. Certainly I expended much energy during our long acquaintance, trying to guess things, searching for suppressed meanings behind what he said, examining his behaviour with care. For however good he was at assuming his customary disguise, his behaviour was sometimes conflicting, and from the conflict sparks flew, pinpricks of light, encouraging the interested person to probe further and gather shreds of evidence until he came up with results.

Despite that, I didn't have a clear picture in my mind, and I only began to suspect that my thoughts and suppositions had some basis in fact during an encounter that I could not conceivably have anticipated. The connection between Shawqi and the wife of the Black Policeman may appear tenuous, but it was in the course of her account of her husband's life that forgotten threads, strands which I had passed over, missing pieces, began to weave together, forming themselves into a whole and finally clarifying my perception of what Shawqi had become.

6

Although Shawqi had taken refuge in his own inexplicable musings when I questioned him, I had previously gleaned some information from long-standing comrades of his whom I had happened to meet at his house. There were vague and obscure areas in the account they gave but I had been able to isolate the main features of the Black Policeman's role in the lives of Shawqi and his fellows. These differed considerably from the stories about his sexual activities published by some newspapers when the fact of his existence had been widely publicized. (This was after the end of the reign of terror when crimes that had been condoned by the former regime were subject to reinvestigation.)

His job had been to beat them up, some of them to make them confess and others just for the sake of it, to break their spirits. He used a variety of instruments – rods, whips, shoes, cudgels, and his bare hands. Although the press had waxed eloquent on the subject of his colour, he wasn't black as they had maintained, but the deep brown of a man from Upper Egypt. Just to see him was frightening because of the aura surrounding him as a result of the repellent stories about him. He was taller than a lot of people, but not extraordinarily tall, and he always seemed to be glorying in himself and his strength, even to his fellow policemen. When he shook hands he would continue to squeeze just for the sake of it until the man he was greeting cried out in pain and fell to his knees. People who had watched him working on his victims said that he did not look human, or even animal; and yet no machine ever had an expression of savage enjoyment as it worked.

They recalled for me the dreaded moment when he arrived at

the wing of the prison where they were kept and his key turned in
the lock. They all knew the sound of it so well and could
distinguish it even in their dreams, starting up when they heard
it, however muffled it was. And every time their hearts turned
over with it. Whose turn was it this time? Then there was the
noise of his footsteps as he crossed the lower courtyard, that
dreadful sound of his tread. How their ears learnt, taught by all-
pervading fear, to be the centre of activity, to develop their role till
they encompassed the mind. So they became able to distinguish
between footsteps going to cell seven on the first floor and those
crossing the courtyard to the stairs up to the next floor. From the
first sound of his foot on the bottom step their ears had to learn to
recognize which floor he was making for and immediately after
that which cell. Then they could prepare themselves either for
dreadful abiding terror, the climax of all the preceding emotion,
or for relief, terrifying too in its own way, and a sigh of thank
God.

It was a dirty way of hitting. In everyday life when two people
fight each other, it's altogether different. The feeling of the one
who's down that he can fight back greatly relieves the impact of
the blow, and the pain issuing from it evaporates instantly,
becoming a spur lending force to his attack. In short, you don't
feel it when you are at liberty to return it.

You felt it in there, when you were obliged to take it but were
denied the right or even the possibility of returning it. In there
you experienced what it really feels like to be hit. Not only the
localized pain and the more general physical pain, but the
accompanying feeling, worse and more pervasive, of humiliation.
Every blow, though it is aimed at a particular part of your body,
affects the whole of you, your sensibilities, your human dignity.
The pain is agonizing because it attacks you from the inside, a
direct hit without the intervention of skin and bone, or the
possibility of recourse to the human right of self-defence.

The right of a person to refuse or accept or counter acts of
aggression against him is an inseparable part of the fabric of his
being, as much as his living flesh. This, and not his clothes or the
walls of his house, protects him and keeps the life-blood of his
humanity flowing through his veins. Yet when it is torn away
from him he does not die the merciful death of a tortoise robbed of

its shell but lives on, unable to protect or defend himself.

How much worse when he is forced to forgo it himself, compelled by brute force to accept pain in silence. Changed into a naked mass of trembling flesh he abandons his humanity and, unable even to bite or kick, his animal instincts too. Silence in the face of pain is more unbearable than pain itself, especially if it is you who must impose silence upon yourself.

The only way to meet the pain and the shame of this kind of attack is to suffer and endure. Suicide may seem like a way out, although it is impracticable or unthinkable for most people, but a distasteful fact about this situation is that you not only suffer and endure, but cling with increasing tenacity on to life. Your last gasp is embarrassingly strong and powerful. Outwardly, you accept the blows raining down on you – brutal, degrading and agonizingly painful – but inside you rage and curse. Feelings of shame and humiliation tear at you and dissolve your spirit with the destructive ferocity of acid poured on it, because you are not dying and do not want to die but cling obsequiously to life.

The most horrible thing was to watch him, this Black Policeman, when he was hitting someone, to see his enjoyment at the destruction of a living creature, a human being, changed before his eyes into a heap of terrified flesh crying out in blind fear. Then you knew that this only encouraged him to take more delight in his task, to hit harder and harder in pursuit of the ultimate pleasure: he had knocked down part of the building and rushed ahead in savage glee to demolish it completely.

The ruin was afraid and in pain, fully aware that it was crashing to the ground, but, with a huge effort of will, not resisting. The aggressor, a wreck of another sort, seemed to rise higher as he was destroyed. The pain he caused in one of his own species made him happy and he revelled in the power of his will, which enabled him to kill all his natural responses to pain. He didn't stop until his victim was on his knees and he was in a state of criminal intoxication, so contemptible that most creatures could not stoop to it, and only a man debased among men could actually enjoy it.

7

We had reached the point in our journey where we could go no
further by car despite all the driver's impressive efforts to keep
going. So we got out, and while the driver stood brushing away
the hordes of children that came and settled on the station wagon,
we three went on our way on foot. Abdullah, still in his slippers,
carrying the file and the case of instruments for the medical
examination, was showing us the way, while Shawqi and I
walked side by side. With every step I grew more curious to see
this black giant – terrorizer of the choice flower of our generation
– in his decline. I had almost forgotten Shawqi and we walked
along in silence, so I welcomed Abdullah's attempts to slacken his
pace for us to catch up with him. He proffered snippets relating to
Abbas and it was obvious that his distaste for the task was waning
fast. Once again he had assumed his preferred role as the
omniscient, and was determined to show us that even when it
came to the Black Policeman, he could tell us things that we did
not know and was ready with advice and information.

'There was a time when he was given more glory than Farouk
himself, sir. He'd come into the county hall and even when he
wasn't in full uniform, they'd salute him and give him the works.
Not a single officer dared to talk to him and remain seated or he
would have been transferred straightaway to some remote
backwater. None of us was man enough to raise our eyes to him –
we were terrified even to look in his direction. Once I swear to
God sir, he dropped some money and didn't even bother to bend
down and pick it up. I remember when I used to see him travel-
ling in the car with the Prime Minister's driver – or even the Prime
Minister himself – he was huge, terrible. Once I swear I saw them
with my own eyes shutting him up with one of the political
prisoners in the room on the second floor of the county hall – the
one directly opposite the medical office. He stayed in there from
first thing in the morning beating him up, and the lad was
screaming, but he wasn't bothered. And when we went home at
five o'clock we left them there still at it . . . .'

'That's enough talk Abdullah . . . where's the house?' I
jumped, and so did Abdullah. Shawqi's voice was abnormally

loud. Never did I remember hearing that note in it before; his words always came out as if he didn't want you to think that it was him speaking. Abdullah was silent at once, and his face took on the look of perfunctory severity which it often wore in front of the young doctors. I looked at Shawqi. He didn't appear angry but he was smiling strangely with the lower part of his face, while the rest of it was transfixed as if intent on some far away voice. I whispered to him:

'What's the matter? What are you thinking about?'

With the same smile, he said:

'Nothing. Should I be?'

I turned my attention once more to the shops we were passing and the children who were clamouring around our little cavalcade, but to my astonishment Shawqi suddenly abandoned his customary dignity and grabbed hold of my arm, pulling me agitatedly in his direction. Like a child who has decided on a sudden impulse to reveal a secret, he whispered in my ear:

'Do you know whom the Black Policeman was hitting there from morning till night? Do you?'

Our eyes met for a split second and I guessed the answer. Laughter shone in his eyes as he confirmed it:

'It was me.'

Again the unexpected occurred, and he let go of my arm and moved towards Abdullah:

'Well then, Abdullah . . . Tell us more. What else have you heard about Abbas al-Zanfali?'

Abdullah looked inquiringly at his boss and became anxious and ill at ease. He did not answer, as if he was scared.

Intently Shawqi goaded him on:

'What else? Tell us more.'

As if Abdullah was at last satisfied that this was a real opportunity, he plunged forth attesting to the truth of what he said by pointing out that sometimes he had seen for himself and sometimes he had heard reports from a friend or a colleague: how the Prime Minister of the time had noticed him on some occasion and taken a fancy to him and made him a member of his bodyguard; how being in close contact with him had made him realize that he was what he had always been looking for, with his great reserves of hardness and lack of emotion, and he had made a present of him to the political police. A handsome present indeed, for among all those entrusted with beating up the political prisoners he was the most brutal and gave of himself the most, not only in carrying out orders but in devising the most efficacious and salutary ways of doing so.

They used to say that he lost all sense of direction and acted drunk or crazy so that they didn't dare to leave him alone with his victims. There always had to be two observers whose job was to intervene at the appropriate time to wrest the accused away from him before he finished him off. This was done only with difficulty, under protest from Abbas, and sometimes they had to join forces to overpower him and tie his hands behind his back. For this reason they always chose two of the strongest policemen, but still there were many occasions when he flared up in anger at them and refused to hand over his victim, directing his blows at them if they tried to stand in his way.

He used to arrive in the morning with the Prime Minister and when he had finished his duties in the prison and the county hall and sometimes very occasionally in the police chief's room itself, he would again ride sitting next to the Prime Minister's driver in the return cortege. He wore a huge revolver in a red holster, and they said that he was like one of the family in the Prime Minister's house. He ate there, and accepted small remunerations from the great lady, and the minister bestowed lavish favours on him, like packets of expensive cigarettes.

They used to say, although whether they had it right or not is another matter, that the Prime Minister himself took an almost ecstatic delight in his splendid upright physique, and considered him a perfect specimen of manhood. He would often order him to be brought before his guests in his drawing-room, especially the foreigners, in order to show him off to them. He would make him stand there displaying his physical attributes and the strength of his muscles, glorying in him as his own special discovery; and how the ladies would sigh . . .

I don't know why Abdullah fell silent at this point. Perhaps he felt he had talked too much, or on unsuitable topics, or his supply of gossip had run out. He may have stolen a glance at the doctor and realized that Shawqi's interest in what he was saying had dropped so much as to be almost non-existent. He was distracted from the company, apparently intent once more on his distant voice.

8

The place where Abdullah made us stop had little in common with any house of my experience. It was unlike poor city housing and yet it was not a village-style dwelling made out of mud bricks. You could have best described it as the missing link between a mud hut and a house, between village and urban building. We had reached it by endless narrow streets and alley-ways; sometimes these took us down steps or forced us to negotiate high heaps of rubble, remains of houses which had decayed and fallen down but had nobody to clear them away, and so had changed into mounds blocking an alley or forming a hillock between two streets.

Abdullah knocked on the door, and then went on knocking for so long without gaining a response that we began to think that there was no one at home. We suggested that we may have come to the wrong house but he assured us that he couldn't possibly be mistaken, and lent weight to his conviction by proceeding to bang on the door with the flat of his hand. At last we fancied that we heard some confused noises from inside the house, whereupon Abdullah's hammering reached such proportions that the door gave way and opened by itself.

Through the doorway we saw a large room which was like the courtyard of a village mayor's house transported to the heart of Cairo. It was empty except for a couch without cushions or a back, like they have in rural areas, which occupied one corner; and more or less in the middle of the room was an upturned washbowl on which stood a hen pecking at the scant traces of dust and earth which clung to the bottom of it. She may have been finding food there, but the only apparent effect of her activity was the regular monotonous tapping of her beak on the washbowl. It rang out insistently, high-pitched and metallic, adding to the desolation of the large empty room.

For a few moments we hesitated, undecided whether to retreat or stand firm, but then a side door opened and through it came a woman. She was slightly built, short and fair-skinned, with deep-set black eyes like the women from the north of the Delta and the Lake District, but the three-cornered tattoo on her chin, just under the lower lip, identified her unmistakably as an Upper Egyptian woman. Her eyes had a spark in them, a hint of allure and sensual passion, but she was emaciated and pale, undoubtedly anaemic, and on her face was a scab the size of a large coin. Her small bare feet were like a child's or a Chinese woman's, and she wore, in the height of summer, a brushed cotton gallabiyya, peasant women's dress, torn in places to reveal a clean yellow nightshirt.

She came through the door as if propelled, in flight from evil, and when she noticed that the outer door was open and saw us, three tall men blocking the doorway, she gasped and immediately withdrew into a second room. We were left standing there, wondering, and again let our eyes rove around the room. The hen, who had been startled by the appearance of the woman, alighted once more on the washbowl and resumed the melancholy regular tapping of her beak.

With a gesture of disgust, Abdullah raised his fist and brought it crashing down on the open door, upsetting the hen and shattering the silence utterly. Agitated himself, his patience exhausted, he shouted: 'Come on out.'

The door opened and the small woman emerged. She had put on a worn black dress and draped the thick cotton garment that she had been wearing around her head. She came towards us, walking uncertainly, saying: 'Please come in.'

Before she reached us Abdullah had told her why we were there and to my surprise I found myself counted as a member of the deputation: he began talking of us as the regional health board in its entirety.

The woman took everything in at a glance. We were obviously not the first such deputation to enter the house, although apparently we were to be the last.

When Abdullah had finished she hung her head submissively and repeated: 'Please come in.'

'Are you his wife?'

'Yes, sir.'

'Where is he?'

'Asleep inside.' And for the third time she repeated: 'Please come in.'

In a peremptory voice, he ordered her: 'You go in front of the gentlemen. Show them the way.'

But instead she stood there, unsure what to do, then said at last, indicating the couch in the corner of the room:

'Just have a seat there for a minute, could you? Just for a minute.'

We didn't know why we should comply with this request but still we found ourselves making our way over to the couch. Whereas I decided to resign myself to the situation and sit down, Shawqi preferred to remain standing and so Abdullah was forced to do the same.

The woman had left us and gone back through the door which she had originally come out of, and we could hear her talking, although no one appeared to be answering her. Then she came out and disappeared into the other room to fetch something which she hid from us in the folds of her dress. Back into the first room she went, then out she came again, and so she went on backwards and forwards between the two rooms, and we followed her with our eyes and did not speak. The hen's regular tapping on the tin bowl was the only sound to break the silence: she was now unruffled by the woman's comings and goings.

At last the woman seemed to have finished, for she came and stood near us. In accusing tones, Abdullah asked her:

'Aren't you ready? The doctors haven't got all day. We've got plenty of other visits still to make.'

She buried her face in her improvised headshawl:

'Yes . . . ready . . . just one minute.'

And Abdullah burst out:

'How long are they, your minutes? Hours? I swear to God they're more like days.'

The woman went on standing there, without moving or speaking. Then suddenly she seemed exhausted and squatted down and sat cross-legged, leaning her back against the wall.

9

We did not have any idea why we had been kept waiting so long, although there must have been a particular reason. We felt constrained by the silence which engulfed us and reached out even to absorb the tapping of the hen's beak; for some reason I took it upon myself to relieve the embarrassment of the situation and put an end to the dismal silence, and so I began to question the wife. I could not have sustained such a conversation for more than a few minutes, consumed as I was by my desire to see the Black Policeman. But although at first when replying to my questions, she gave quick short answers, preceded by a rapid, embarrassed search of my features as if to guess at my intentions, these answers began to command my attention, and Shawqi's too.

I had realized, although no word passed between us, that Shawqi was as eager as I was to see Abbas. He was visibly annoyed when I began to ask questions and, as he saw it, wasted time by opening the way for a conversation to start up. But then he himself began to take notice and followed our exchange compulsively, almost joining in but always holding himself back at the last minute.

And so a quarter of an hour passed. Nur, the wife, began to be upset by the questions, crying as she answered them, but I persisted until we came through that stage and she answered openly, as if she wanted to empty her heart of its undisclosed pain. Or perhaps she genuinely believed that she could alleviate the harshness of the decision that we were about to pronounce on her husband's fate.

So it was that my interest in gleaning whatever information I could from Nur surpassed my curiosity to see her husband. And I was not alone. All three of us listened to her; we forgot our impatience, we were no longer aware of time passing, and did not give a thought to the man lying in the next room. She too seemed to be infected by our interest, and abandoned her present concerns to become wholly absorbed in the past.

Of course the story as I had it from her differed considerably from the account which Abdullah had volunteered and represented quite a different picture from the one formed by Shawqi, and all those who had suffered at Abbas' hands in prison. It was the story of a peasant who acquired fame in his village when he grew up to be stronger and more powerfully built than his fellows. This strength bestowed authority upon him, and had its perquisites, not the least of which was a silk gallabiyya and shawl. Displaying himself proudly in this suit of finery at the time of the afternoon prayer, he took the market-place by storm. He sat with the men in their councils, and dazzled the eyes of the young girls and divorced women; he charmed her, his cousin, the most beautiful of them all. It was the old story of machismo – taking bets on the number of bales of cotton or sacks of fertilizer he could carry, flying into passionate rages, fighting and playing at duelling with long sticks. And still, as she said, how happy she had been to marry him, and she had been ready to wait, not only for the five years of his military service, but for the rest of her life if necessary. He came, eventually, after his time in the army and took her, and lived with her in Cairo.

They had always lived here in this house which time had not changed one bit. He got a job in the police force. True he had not blessed her with children, a worry which had nagged at him and upset him. But her joy in him had always surpassed any deprivation or cruelty that she had suffered at his hands, and had made up for the lack of offspring. Once he had taken her to the doctor and, finding no defect in her, the doctor had said to him have yourself looked at. But he had always been too busy running after power and authority, or quarrelling with his bosses and trying to better himself at the expense of his colleagues. Until eventually he was rewarded when the Pasha took him up and he got the post that seemed like the gateway to happiness.

Not a day went by when he came home without a basket of meat and vegetables. Laughter rang out in the room until bedtime. The house was crowded with people and there were always parties that lasted till past midnight. The whole neighbourhood knew about his important position. Most of them saw him sitting proudly in the front of the Pasha's car. Not long after he had started arriving home in it, and the neighbours had seen him with their own eyes, gloriously aloft, the jealous Umm Ali with her evil eye came to her to describe the gasps of envy and wonder that followed him wherever he went, in the car or on foot.

She advised Nur to protect her husband by uttering incantations over him, and when she followed this counsel it was the evil eye of Umm Ali that Nur sought to ward off first.

She got up at dawn to pray, begging God to preserve them from people who meant them harm, and to exempt them by his grace from their affairs being exposed to public scrutiny. There was a constant stream of callers, and from strangers and friends and family alike came petitions, complaints, requests for jobs and promotion, even – the irony of it – pleas addressed to Abbas that he should intervene before the Pasha to gain the release of internees.

Abbas received them all and did what he could for them with the exception of these latter. He upbraided those who approached him on such matters, and sometimes informed against them to the political police. Only in one case of this nature did he ever agree to act: they were surprised by a visit from the chief magistrate of their own village, an official personage, Ahmad Bey Marwan. He, accompanied by his aged father and a huge delegation from the Marwan family, knocked on the door of their house, this very house, and drank their coffee, and addressed himself to Abbas, calling him sir, and officer, and God bless you sir. He even got as far as kissing his hand. Nur saw him herself through the door which stood ajar: he grasped hold of Abbas' hand, bent low over it and vowed by all that he held sacred that he would kiss it. After that what could Abbas do but promise that he would make every effort to plead with the Pasha to secure the release of Basyuni, the magistrate's brother, a student who had been interned. He succeeded, and Marwan presented him with a sheep and fifty pounds cash, the most he had ever had in his pocket at one time, although he would be slipped a certain amount with each petition.

He spent the money riotously, always moving in a group from the neighbourhood or from his native village. They were always around him, keeping him company in the cafe, or at home, meeting together in this same big room each evening. Full, fruitful days, yet nothing was left from them, all trace of past glory gone, except two hundred pounds in the post office.

And after all they had not lasted long, these days of fortune. Try as she might, in response to importunate questioning, Nur could not define precisely what had happened, or when. At first all that she had noticed was that when the visitors had left and he was no longer surrounded by his friends, and the house was empty save for him and her, all joy and laughter went from him. He sat where he was, cross-legged on the floor, with his head bowed low, bemused by a sudden sadness, which she did not understand. There he would stay for an hour or more, not moving, not talking to her or changing his position except at long intervals when he would suddenly raise his head and let out a deep sigh, saying:

'Ah well . . . that's life.'

Then his head would drop forward again and he would revert to his former state of sad distraction.

Even if this went on for some time and she was emboldened to ask what was the matter with him, she was never rewarded with an answer. Or if he raised his head it was only to say, 'It doesn't matter. It'll all be sorted out soon.'

She was sure that there was no question of another woman and they weren't short of money, and so she didn't insist, and would fall silent, especially while he wasn't like it often. But then it happened more frequently, nearly every night, and went on for longer. Abbas stayed later and later at work, and then came back looking as if someone had assaulted him physically. He went to bed without eating anything, or if he did eat and she went to bed before him she would wake up to the strangled sound of his voice, crying out in a nightmare.

Then came the horrors with opium. She knew that he used to take it, but that was just to get a little kick, nothing more. But as his fits of depression increased and his work took up more and more of his time, he started to depend on it until he was hooked. He took it all the time – before he slept, in the middle of the night, and even before breakfast on an empty stomach. If she opened her mouth to protest, he would give her a look that made her quail before him and swallow her words, but inside her she was in a fever of anxiety, eaten up with fear of him, and for him.

She would put his supper in front of him and come back to find it just as she had left it, then he would sleep. He began coming home only to sleep, and couldn't bear to be in the house alone when he was awake. When he was going to bed he would ask her to wake him early, but when she called him he would shout insults at her, and if she kept trying he would half kill her, cowing her into silence so that he could go on sleeping.

The day came when he no longer went to the café, and he gave her instructions to tell his friends that he was not in if they called at the house asking for him. Every time she was faced with a new symptom, she would tell herself that it was just a phase and it would pass. But rather than reverting to his former self he changed daily for the worse. Her only hope then was that he would just go back to being as he had been the day before, and, when she despaired even of that, simply that he would not deteriorate any further.

She accepted him as he was: always scowling, angry, impatient, ready to flare up for the most trivial reason, or for no reason at all. He no longer provided for her or for the household needs, and in spite of all that he earned, the wallet under his pillow was empty; the money squandered, sunk without trace. He wandered aimlessly, going nowehere in particular but further away from her, and from everyone. He didn't greet people in the street, as if the action cost him too much or they were his enemies to be shunned at all cost. Every day some incident occurred: he swore at somebody or had a fight with the neighbour or the greengrocer's delivery boy, or a cyclist who had rung his bell at him, until eventually he seemed to be at odds with almost all the world and it was unanimously agreed that the best course was to keep away from him.

If he tired of his own company and his solitary existence on some occasions, and sent for his friends to come, they did so under duress. They sat listening to his conversation as a duty grudgingly assumed, for it was filled with accounts of situations in which he was the hero, and stories in which he inevitably broke some detainee's arm at a blow or smashed another's teeth in. And then it was what the Prime Minister said to him and what he replied; and if he noticed a trace of sympathy on the features of one of his listeners, or if a word of criticism was uttered against the government's actions, he seized the opportunity to speak, without subtlety, about the government, and the Prime Minister, and the recent agreement, as if he were directly involved. He would constantly be saying ' we did so-and-so', or 'we had to take

such-and-such action', and describing the political prisoners and
the dissidents as 'our enemies'. The gathering did not last long as
people would soon begin to drift away, one after the other,
offering excuses, mostly feeble, and he would sit there after they
had gone, cursing them, and people and life in general. He talked
to himself, a rare occurrence in the beginning, although it had
become common by that time, and whether he was in the living-
room or the other room, she would hear him talking, sometimes
shouting, and cursing and groaning aloud: 'Aah, yes, they're all
the same. That's the way it is damn it. To hell with the lot of
them, to hell . . .'

Nur couldn't say how or when she had begun to notice that
Abbas was a changed man, although the realization had stunned
her. He was a stranger with traits of character that were entirely
unfamiliar to her. She found it hard to accept that he was the
same man that she had married, and it was obvious that for his
part, even though he had cut off all his former acquaintances and
she was the only one left to him, he had begun to find her strange
and reject her; he no longer cherished tender feelings towards
her, nor cared where she got money from or how she managed.

Umm Ali of the evil eye told her that it was opium that had
changed him, but she, by now an expert in her knowledge of him,
realized that opium, like his impatience, or his air of distraction,
or the way he shunned company, was an effect and not a cause;
the cause was too great or too remote for her to comprehend
alone. But they had always lived like any of God's creatures,
trusting in his loving care, so what had gone wrong?

She said to herself that it must be the evil eye, Umm Ali's in
particular. She burnt incense and recited charms and made an
effigy of her and gouged out its eyes. Then she went to the shaykh
of the amulets and paid the fee and sacrificed the black cock, in
short tried all the remedies and cures, but things only grew worse.
He continued to avoid her in bed; it was as if a spell had been put
on him, preventing him from making love to her. She tried insistently to make him let go, and she succeeded, but afterwards he
was still a stranger. If it had not been that he still looked the
same, she would not have known him, and he continued to grow
away from her and was hardly aware of her existence, or else
chose to ignore it.

One of the worst nights of all was when she decided to stand up for herself, drop her veil of diffidence and confront him. Now she wished that she had not been so imprudent. He had stood listening in silence until she was completely drained of all expression but her tears, and so she wept. Instead of Abbas, her husband and her uncle's son, a wild thing had borne down on her, burying his nails in her flesh, gripping her with both hands and replying to what she had said with the filthiest, foulest phrases she had ever heard in her life. Words that he had never used before that night, that she would not have believed him capable of knowing, let alone giving voice to. What had stopped him hitting her, why he had not pulverized her with his great fist and killed her outright, she would never know, since for far less he had not held back. She was convinced that fate must have wanted her to have a second chance.

It was as if he had been waiting for an opportunity to push matters to a head, to force things to such a pitch that she would actually contemplate running away, although she would have had to walk the streets, for had she gone back to the village in anger she would have faced certain death. She thought and planned and began to watch him in order to decide exactly the right moment to go.

By that time he was acting like a madman: he would wake up screaming in terror, or she would come upon him suddenly sitting alone, swearing and hurling abuse at himself, using the same obscene phrases that he had used to her before. When once she saw him actually assaulting himself physically, raising his hand to strike his own face, she decided that the time had come to get out as quickly as she could.

But in the event things were to turn out differently. One day Abbas returned home from work much earlier than usual, before noon, and slept. He slept on into the following day but before he lay down she had heard him muttering something to her. She had been afraid to ask him to repeat it, but while he was asleep some of her neighbours came in and told her that the Pasha whom Abbas had worked with had left office, and they were holding elections to choose a new Pasha. When Abbas woke up, she tried to start a conversation so that she could tell him the news, but he didn't respond. He dissolved a piece of opium and swallowed it down, then gave her a piece of paper and told her where to take it, and went back to sleep.

The piece of paper was a request for sick leave, although she wasn't to know that it was to be the first of a never-ending succession of official forms.

Nur was still sitting cross-legged near the couch. She spoke disjointedly and the place seemed almost to vibrate with the anguished ring of truth in her soft hoarse voice. Shawqi followed her words feverishly, moving compulsively nearer the edge of the couch, his head bent low near hers to catch every word, all trace of aloofness leaving him as he began to listen. He enclosed the woman in his gaze, his piercing eyes like needles, trying to pluck out of her everything that she couldn't bring herself to say, or was incapable of expressing, and from time to time he fired a direct question at her. Even Abdullah was so gripped by what she was saying that he put formality aside and sat cross-legged next to her listening. On numerous occasions he tried unsuccessfully to shoo the hen away by gesturing irritably with his hand, never turning his head.

Before she had finished her story, when we still did not know what exactly had happened to him or what form his most recent illness had taken, there was a sudden terrible sound. I don't remember being thoroughly frightened since I was a child and believed in hobgoblins and haunted houses. Of course I have felt uneasy and my heart has quickened with some vague feeling of fear, but never that same terror. I was so frightened I wanted to run. It was a scream, or so we thought at first, but then it kept coming. The nature of it changed, and it became like a howling. If we'd been out in the wilds we would have thought it was a wolf, and not been afraid. But we were in the heart of Cairo, inside a house, and although the noise was a wolf howling, you knew that it was coming from a man, not mimicking a wolf in fun, but giving voice to some spiritual agony, wresting it out of himself in a long drawn out howling, indistinguishable from a wolf's howl.

I was not the only one to take fright. When I came to my senses I found that I was on my feet and so were the others, wide-eyed and full of dread. But the woman, showing no such signs, was the first to move and leaving us frozen there, hurried towards the door of the room where the sound had come from, like a mother to her suckling child. As soon as she went in the sound came again but stopped abruptly, suddenly cut off. It was followed by a rising sob, a little harsh, but still you might have thought it came from a child.

Abdullah, imploringly, almost weeping, said, 'Why not leave him, doctor – for the boss . . . please, I want to.'

I noticed Shawqi blench, his eyes roving from the door, to Abdullah, to me, confused.

At that very moment I was going through the state of shame that often follows on after fear, when we are embarrassed, as grown-up men, to have felt paralyzing fear, and the sense of this shame drives us to scorn what has frightened us and rush in to challenge it. It seemed that, reading this in my eyes, Shawqi was trying his utmost to assure me that he was not afraid either and that we must see our task through to the end. And so it was that we went into the room.

It had grown late. Whether it was past sunset, or the sun was still about to sink below the horizon, we couldn't tell, for the room was lit only by a tiny window near the ceiling, like a prison cell. When we entered we could see almost nothing and to us it looked like a storeroom full of old forgotten shadows; our ears alone were able to function, picking up the stifled sobs rising and falling in the heavy air.

We were disconcerted for a moment or two, then we found that we could see, so easily that it seemed our eyes must have over-reacted, blinded only as we entered. The room was spacious, like the one we had been in, with little furniture: a mat covering the floor, a well-worn old bride's cupboard in one corner, and on the right a four-poster bed with a mattress and pillows whose torn ticking and dirty cotton covers were plainly visible. The atmosphere was close and stuffy so you were loath to breathe, and gasped for breath instead.

Abbas al-Zanfali was half-lying on the bed, supported by his wife; he looked as if he had just stopped crying. It isn't easy for me to describe his condition. One would expect a sick person to show signs of weakness and emaciation, his physical appearance to be changed radically in some way; these manifest signs of illness were there in Abbas but were insignificant in comparison with the look in his eyes. In a sick body, the sickness of the eyes shows in the way they glitter, the more brightly because of the pallor of the skin and the gauntness of the frame; and when a man goes mad the unreason in his thoughts shows in his eyes and they are wild, uncontrolled by his will. But Abbas' eyes were not sick or deranged, they were still and unmoving, like death. And there was a completeness about them. Looking at them was like standing on the seashore unable to believe that the vast endless sea breaks somewhere on another shore; their immeasurable stillness was like the surface of the sea in a world without wind or time.

Unsurely, Abdullah greeted Abbas, and the inappropriateness of his gesture was the more apparent since Abbas, who may not even have been aware of our presence, made no effort to reply.

Ever since we had come into the room and my eyes had grown accustomed to the light, I found that my attention was focused on Shawqi at least as much as on Abbas. While he was listening to Nur, and then when he was in the same room as Abbas, faced with tangible proof of his existence, a change had come over him. I had not so much noticed his unprecedented state of mind, as experienced an abrupt revelation. It was something that had always been there but because I had grown so used to seeing it, I had been unconscious of its implications. It was just like not realizing that someone is always miserable until he smiles unexpectedly, or not appreciating a well-satisfied disposition until its owner flares up in resentment. Suddenly Shawqi's conflicting emotions – hesitation, curiosity, astonishment, fear – began to take shape, and his facial muscles responded accordingly. His eternal smile fell away from him and with the veil removed, life began to return to him violently.

Only then did I realize – and how much it surprised me to find out – that my supposition had been correct, my misgivings not unfounded, and the Shawqi I had been around with all those years since he had come out of prison was not the same person that I'd known before. Now, in a flash, he had re-emerged, aggressive, alive and well, as if he had merely been embalmed for a time, in the painted smile perhaps. In retrospect I saw the smile as a dead part of a living face, or as a feature, if stared at concentratedly, which appeared to be the last vestige of a person who

was otherwise dead. Abbas' eyes were what it reminded me of:
frozen and still without a flicker of life, like the surface of the sea
in a world without wind, unbroken by a wave.

I was aware of an onrush of almost overpowering joy, despite
the thoughts and feelings revolving in my head, for I imagined
that Shawqi was sloughing off the pain and fear and coming back.
Surely now I would leave the room in the company of the person
whom I had despaired of ever bringing back to life.

I began to follow events with more passionate involvement.
Now as I try to record what happened I bring back the picture
and slow it down so that I can select details of it and examine
them carefully. I can control the time element and make the
images follow on one after the other. But at the time I was not in
control: things happened in quick succession and I could hardly
keep up with them, let alone keep them in perspective and apply
some rational criteria to distinguish the horror worth recording
from the superficial and less noteworthy events.

With no trace of apprehension or discomfiture Shawqi strode
towards Abbas' bed. As if he could see again after years of blind-
ness, he looked at him, his eyes hard and searching, unafraid.
Any tremulousness in them was there only because Abdullah and
I were looking on. He showed no hatred or resentment, no signs
of relishing Abbas' situation, but looked at him simply as if to
leave no area obscure or unobserved. In a tone of voice that I had
never heard him use before, he said:

'You're Abbas . . .'

The moribund glance that the skeleton of a man turned on
Shawqi, without raising his head, registered a certain impression,
a quickening of interest and of understanding.

'What's the matter with you?'

Shawqi spat it out as if the turmoil inside him was a furnace
fiercely burning, and still the man did not move from his position,
half-lying, half-sitting, but he must have heard.

'Abbas Mahmud al-Zanfali?'

He roared it at him, and again he bellowed:

'Talk.'

I had never heard him raise his voice like this, never seen him
lose his self-control, and my growing delight at him began to be
mixed with some apprehension at the turn which things might

take – Shawqi looked capable of lashing out at the man without warning, kicking him, hitting him, grabbing hold of him by the throat. I tried to intervene, remonstrating with him, begging him to remember what he was there for and observe the ethics proper to a doctor treating a patient, but he took no notice, apparently quite unaware that I had spoken. He seemed to have gone mad with a sort of thwarted ecstasy, presented as he was with this chance of a lifetime.

Abbas' wife spoke: 'Be gentle with him, doctor . . . he's ill.'

'Are you Abbas al-Zanfali?'

The man raised his head and let his stony eyes rest on Shawqi's face, taking the full force of the stream of words which burst anguished from him, from old deep wounds which the passage of time had not eased.

'Don't pretend to be stupid. Don't act as if you've forgotten. Don't you remember the cells, the five o'clock beatings, the room on the ninth floor? The rods and the whip? The blood? Where's your whip, where've you put it? You monster, why aren't you shouting now? Where are your boots with the metal toe-caps? What about your fist, and those fingers of yours? The fire? Look at me and say something. Shout like you used to. Let's hear your voice. Shout, Black Policeman. Look at me and say something. Don't act as if you've forgotten, or I'll do something that'll make you remember. Now. I'll make you remember.'

In that split second Shawqi's jacket and shirt were off and his vest raised to show his bare back. Nowhere on it was there any sign of healthy unbroken skin. An ugly scar ran the length and breadth of it sometimes erupting in raised sores, and in other places gaping wide and deep. It made your flesh creep, not only to see it, but to picture the savage ferocity that had caused it. Some wolfish demon digging its claws and teeth into his back and tearing it to pieces.

He swung round to show Abbas, shouting all the time:

'Even if you've forgotten me, you won't be able to forget this.'

As suddenly as he had begun exposing his back, he stopped, and turned back to him, still shouting:

'Just think about it, so you don't forget again. I haven't forgotten. Nor has anybody else, and no one's going to forget. Speak. Say something. Shout – tell me that you remember. Come on.'

I was scared by what was happening. Shawqi's shouting dis-
quieted me as it grew increasingly loud and high-pitched. The
words became incomprehensible, indistinguishable from one
another. They lost their identity as words and merged into an
uninterrupted stream of sound, of weeping and crying out,
perhaps expressing rage or pain, we couldn't tell. Then the
stream became contorted and was transfigured into a howling,
shuddering and desperate, the sort of sound only made by a living
creature in the final throes of agony beyond the limits of
endurance, when the whole body, and not just the lungs, is
screaming with pain.

We three – myself, Abdullah and the wife – were transfixed at
the sight of Shawqi, convinced that we could do nothing to stop
him. Abbas kept his dead eyes fixed on him and never moved a
muscle, but then, when Shawqi began to howl, a glimmer of
understanding flashed across the surface of them. Then they
trembled violently and a look of alarm came into them which
deepened rapidly into terror that sent currents down into his
body, activating it into life. He drew back, edging towards his
wife, far off at the foot of the bed, and as he went he seemed to
shrink and curl up. Never would I have imagined that a person
could make himself so small: it was as if, had he continued at the
same rate, he would have disappeared altogether, a little ball of
humanity that had simply ceased to exist. Perhaps it was the very
fact that he recoiled in fear that made Shawqi keep coming at him
relentlessly, growing larger as he dwindled, bearing down on him
as he retreated, screaming at him and never pausing for breath as
he climbed on the bed in pursuit of him. Perhaps, on the other
hand, it was this very fear that somehow inhibited Shawqi and
stopped him pouncing on him and crushing the life out of him.

Abbas reached the wall and clung to it, unable to go back any
further; then he opened his mouth and let out the noise we had
heard from the other room. The wailing of the two men rose up in
concert, until Abbas' cries prevailed, and Shawqi fell silent.
Then, surprisingly, a long mouth separated itself from the
shrunken human mass and, thrusting itself this way and that,
began baying like a cornered dog. It stretched out, ready to bite
Shawqi's shoulder, and he took fright, and appeared to return to
his senses. With one bound he was off the bed and out of reach.

The gaping mouth fastened on to the hand of the wife close by, apparently bent on devouring it. She suffered it for a moment or two, begging him to stop, but then suddenly, as if she realized that her hand was on the point of being torn to pieces, she let out a scream, louder than any of the noises that had gone before, followed by a series of shrieks which brought the neighbours hammering on the door. Some of them, a handful of men and women with some children hanging on behind, forced the door and came into the room. But although there were so many people gathered round by now, not one of us dared approach Abbas to free Nur's hand from the mouth clamped over it, and she only got away when the mouth opened of its own volition to shout again.

She joined us tearfully, and we all stood some distance away from the bed watching what happened. Abbas had begun to strike the bed, still crying out, and to bite and claw at the mattress. His fury increased and he beat his face with his palms like a woman lamenting, and dragged his nails down his cheeks, tearing the skin. With every second that passed we expected him to calm down, but he didn't, and it must have crossed the mind of each one of us to get out, fearing for his own safety.

It was then that Abbas, staring at us with wild burning eyes, brought his jaws together on the flesh of his own skinny arm, which protruded from the sleeve of his torn nightshirt. As he sunk his teeth in further his saliva ran all over his bare forearm, and either he didn't feel the pain or else it made him madder, and he bit deeper. It was obvious what must happen, and the women turned their faces away, and we turned ours with them.

Only Shawqi, I noticed, did not turn away: he stood watching in an attitude of horrified fascination. When we turned back we found that we had not avoided very much. Although Abbas had raised his face from his arm, blood fell from his mouth mixed with his saliva: his lips were drawn back to reveal his teeth and clenched between them was the piece of bloody flesh that he had torn from his arm. An ugly exposed wound had appeared on his arm in the place where it had come from. He still wailed, in a strangulated voice because of having something between his teeth; it seemed as if his voice was bleeding and the blood stifling his howls.

A framed certificate hanging on the wall by the bed suddenly

caught my eye, its burnished letters glinting under the dirty glass.
Strange as it may seem, I found myself becoming oblivious to
what was going on around me as I looked at it. It was a government service award, second class, bearing the testimonial that I
had already seen quoted in the file on Shawqi's desk. This time I
was particularly struck by the words '. . . his self-sacrifice in the
service of the highest interests of the nation'.

That was the last either of us ever saw of the Black Policeman
as Shawqi left the writing of the report on him to his boss. I could
not begin to surmise in the days that followed what effect that
meeting had made upon him but, with my hopes kindled by what
I had seen in those few minutes when he had seemed to revert to
his former self, I devised schemes for resuming my efforts with
him, helped by the fact that he seemed obsessed with the subject
and brought it up on every conceivable occasion.

Once he said: 'Do you know that when you hurt somebody else
you hurt yourself without realizing it?' And another time, with a
short laugh: 'Let the torturer carry on torturing. He'll end up
turning on himself.'

Not only did he think about it: I came in one day to find him
reading avidly. As soon as he saw me he bundled the papers
away, but between his fingers I could make out a few headings:
'The Philosophy of Torture', 'The Infliction of Pain as a Double-
Edged Weapon', and others similar. When I asked him about it,
he said that it was some research that he would show me one day.

I had only to talk with Shawqi a few more times after that to
realize that what I had witnessed in Abbas' room was nothing
more than a brief recovery of consciousness before death. The
change in him was irreversible: normal healthy skin could not
grow again in place of the scars that covered his back. I had
finally grasped what had escaped me all these years: that Shawqi,
having once lost his sense of security as a human being, could
never retrieve it and become one of us again.

Every time I went back over all that had happened the same
few words stuck in my mind, although they had seemed quite
unremarkable at the time. It was when we were all on our way
out of the room, unable to bear the sight of the lump of flesh
between Abbas' teeth and the blood which seemed to taint things
wherever we looked. I heard one of the women, perhaps Umm Ali

of the evil eye herself, sucking in her lips disparagingly, and whispering to her neighbour:

'Human flesh, dear. Once a man tastes it he always wants more. And if he can't get hold of anything else, he'll even eat his own, God help us all.'

The words meant nothing to me at the time, an old wives' tale to be mocked and forgotten. I don't know why they should keep coming back to me.

The Siren

⊂⊃⊂⊃⊂⊃⊂⊃

When Hamid pushed open the door and was suddenly confronted
by the dreadful scene, everything in him stopped, he died. He felt
himself immobilized, every thought, every tremor of emotion in
him silenced, and he could no longer see or hear or feel. The
world about him subsided too, and died, and everything was
finished.

Fathiyya, his wife, was lying on the floor of the room, and the
little boy, sobbing in terror, was hanging on to her hair, pulling it
vehemently, for her head was bare, like her legs and thighs, and
almost all of her, and on top of her lay a man in a jacket, but
without trousers or underpants, and his bare behind had melted
into Fathiyya's nakedness and it was all over.

It was a silent spectacle bathed in the gloom of noontide which
settled familiarly about the room. No sign of resistance disturbed
it, no sound at all until, what seemed like a year later, there came
a dreadful sobbing intake of breath, startled, fearful, expressive of
the profoundest horror: 'Hamid!'

At the sound of it the child started in fright and began to
scream aloud, but no one heard him: life drained away from the
room and even the dark shadows paled, partaking of the desolation all around – and another year passed by. The first to move
was the Man. With one bound he had pulled up his trousers and
was outside the room, and with another his trousers were in their
proper place and he had left the building.

Whereupon Hamid moved, because the renewed life in him
came not to his mind, but to his legs. He too left, first the room,
then the building, in a series of leaps, as if his life depended on
them; but he was still one jump behind. When he got out into the
street the Man had become ten or twenty men, all of them in
jackets, and all of them with behinds which were covered by
trousers, and most of them bounding along at full speed, all in
different directions.

Then as his mind began to work again, he realized that he had followed the Man in the Suit involuntarily, compelled to jump in his wake, and that the object of his attention was properly his wife: it could almost be narrowed down in her to that particular part of a woman that builds and destroys houses and causes bitter feuds, mankind's heaven and hell and refuge from the world.

So he turned back, this time without excitement. He raised one foot and seemed almost to keep it suspended in mid-air, for his newly revived mind would only work like the mind of a small child faced with a problem, and his problem in this instance was that he was afraid. He certainly intended to go back home – to the room – but there was not in his whole being one atom of desire to confront a wife whose lower half was naked, her body still bearing traces of the man's bestiality upon it, and marked by his imprint.

It was his fear eventually which drove him back to her. Of the many feelings that came and went in the space of a few moments, the bitterest and most powerful was one of betrayal: not only did he feel that Fathiyya, and the Man, had betrayed him, but the whole of creation. Little children rush to their mothers for comfort when the world lets them down, depending on them to restore their faith in existence, and men expect their wives to do the same. So what if the source of betrayal is the mother – or the wife – herself? That was Hamid's dilemma, and he was pitiable, pulled this way and that in agony, torn between a desire to run away and never see her again, and a desire to rush to her and fling himself on her breast and pour out his troubles to her, even if she was the cause of them.

He felt that Fathiyya, his woman, his wife, his female half, the person whom he had known as he had known and been sure of his own right hand, of his masculinity and of his very decency, had changed. A strange creature had shuddered into life from out of her, she was transformed into a wild thing who played false with him then attacked him from behind while he submitted willingly, still trusting. A wild thing of whom he was so excessively frightened that he was driven panic-stricken straight into her arms.

If he had killed her on the spot – and the idea had been growing since his mind had first begun to work again, if not before – if he had killed her, it wouldn't have been because of her infidelity or in defence of his threatened honour, or in a sudden frenzy of rage and annoyance. All these would have entered into it, but it would have been rather from a terrible onrush of fear of her, and he had known the feeling many times before. Kill the spotted snake before she kills you, kill her, not to defend your honour but your life first of all. Stop the breath of the creature that took you by surprise when you were innocent and unsuspecting, and savaged you and betrayed you. To betray is to kill, and the only safeguard against one who would kill you is to kill him. And sometimes you have to do more. Sometimes the agonizing sense of a disruption of the natural order can only be assuaged by dealing with the rupture on the spot, burying alive the freak of nature that caused it. The world is no longer a safe place. A yawning gap has suddenly appeared in the kingdom of heaven and earth and if you don't hurry to block it up the jaws of eternity will close around you, you and the whole rotten world.

He was genuinely afraid, so much so that he had begun to tremble, the violence of it making his teeth chatter; more and more he became aware of the deadly impact of the blow, for the hand that held the knife knew his secrets and had struck him where he was most vulnerable. But he still did not feel pain, numb as he was from the first shock of the knife's thrust, and he felt instead the deep open hole that the knife had left behind. When he looked into it he grew dizzy, seeing in the depths of this wound his ending, in an uproar of noise and confusion.

Fathiyya, with her first abrupt movement, felt that she was like thousands of pieces of broken glass reassembling themselves and taking shape. But she did not succeed in raising her body and was only just able to reach out with her hand and grasp the low narrow bedhead. After that, she had intended to run out of the room, or stand up or sit up, or to gather her clothes about her by degrees and cover up her nakedness. This last was all that she managed, with Hamid standing in the doorway holding on to the catch and looking for the first time at the child who had gone silent and thrown himself down on the ground and appeared to be asleep.

There they remained, motionless, he standing holding on to the door, and she, body sprawled, legs apart, gripping on to the bedhead for support; from the way he stared at the child it seemed as if he had become the most important thing to him. She looked up at the ceiling, but saw only Hamid's eyes. In his mind's eye, since his faculties had returned to him, was emblazoned one picture alone, which refused to fade: the Man's bare behind, and the nakedness of Fathiyya fused into a single white mass. She saw only Hamid's expression as she had seen it since the moment she had discovered his presence, and in her head it had taken on the dimensions of a nightmare which almost made her cry out loud for help; in it she saw his eyes changed to fiery swords coming at her without mercy to stab her.

All the difference between them was that Hamid – as usually happened – was trying to see how to take the initiative. Whatever the deadly effect of the shock, the knife-thrust, he knew he must end his dazed contemplation and act, for any further delay would negate his action and make it worthless. Whereas for her it was all over: things had reached their appointed end, and what was always doomed to happen, the event she had feared all her life, had happened. What remained was the punishment, and how thankful she would be if Hamid acted quickly. If he took his time, she might begin to think, and the cruellest punishment on earth would be a thousand times easier to bear than a situation in which she was forced to consider what had happened and relive the events in her mind.

The idea of killing her had thrust itself upwards from the recesses of Hamid's mind to the surface so that he couldn't ignore it, looming large now, ripe for execution. If he killed her, the worst that could happen was a year in prison, perhaps less, or they could even decide that he was innocent. So should he kill her now, take his heavy stick, that he called his cudgel, from its place under the bed and batter her brains out with it?

Should he do it now . . . now . . . or interrogate her first? Or not do it at all? The question, dreadful and insistent, reverberated through his thoughts. The first galling sensation that had all but stopped his breath, the first stupendous shock, deadly, then enlivening, had passed. Now while his image of the scene was as clear as ever, he was confused and angry as he turned over the idea of killing her in his mind, for it seemed irrelevant.

It was as if he were on a railway track with the train approaching fast and all he could do was think about the medicine that the doctor had prescribed for him, and whether it was better to take it before or after meals. He didn't wish for her death at that moment, any more than he wanted her to live, but that was unimportant in comparison with the searing pain which dogged him on his own account. It was this gaping wound which reached into the void, this rush of blood which roared inside him, gathering momentum, bringing him at a frightening pace closer to the end. He saw it approaching fast, felt that he, as he knew himself, would soon be obliterated; and yet it was treacherous, this unexpected ending, still lying in wait for him beyond the next moment while his feeble stupid mind refused to shift a hairsbreadth from its obsession: should he kill her? Or should he wait till she'd confessed, for he knew very well that he'd be unable to kill a fly just then, but that if he waited any longer he'd be fit for nothing, finished.

Strangely enough, it was this concern with the end that was uppermost in Fathiyya's mind at the same time. But the end that she was facing held no fears for her, none of the mounting terror of annihilation that made Hamid tremble. On the contrary, she was lying there anticipating it, longing for it, and the important thing was that it should come straight away, to deliver her before she found herself compelled to think, or especially before she was forced to behold again the expression in Hamid's eyes. Just as he was clinging desperately on to life so that it did not slip away from him while he was still trying to confront the situation, so she, with all the desire for life that was in her, was longing for that life to end so that she would die before anything else happened.

Either a sudden quick death or a miracle she wanted. A miracle would be preferable, so that she could wipe away everything that had happened, rub it out so that it would look as if it had never been there. Life could go back to being as it had been an hour before. Or to be exact, a month before. No, it would have to be as it had been five years before, before she had started to be aware of the voices inside her.

She was ready to fill the Nile with tears, to weep and ask mercy from now till Judgement Day in order not even that God would forgive her, and blot out all that had happened, but just that he would let her and Hamid live for one day, an hour, a few seconds, Lord, as if none of it had happened. How painful then was her knowledge that this could never be, that the die had been cast long before, what had happened had happened, and destiny was fulfilled.

For, to add to her misery, it had come as no surprise to her: she had seen it all with her own two eyes at intervals over the past five years, and particularly during the last dreary year. The idea of it had drawn her, and pursued her, and the voice had whispered to her, and she had foreseen every detail: not the same Man in the Suit, but a Man in a Suit, horizontal, with his trousers off, and the door being pushed open and Hamid coming in. Because she had seen it all and been convinced that it was going to happen in reality, she had behaved as if she were used to it when it did happen, as if the whole scenario had been enacted many times before. No part of the action was unexpected or different from her prognostication of it. The Man in the Suit was always lying in wait for her, observing her in her busy daily round, one child at her breast and the other on her shoulders tugging at her hair and demanding food, and her hands occupied with the cooking on the stove, and her mind with planning her winter dress or deciding what she must get in for Ramadan. Suddenly he would spring out at her, naked from the waist down, crouch over her suddenly so that she almost died of fright, then next moment the door would open and Hamid would be standing there, just as he was now.

So did she have psychic powers? Since her vision of the future had come true, did this prove that she was a saint, a holy woman, when all inside her had seemed to have become perverted and depraved?

The thing was beyond her, and caused her mind to wander, so that she was unable to clarify to herself the nature of her guilt, if indeed she was guilty. She had always reassured herself, whenever the voice had whispered to her and drawn the picture for her, with the thought that she would resist to the death before she would let anybody touch her, be he an ordinary mortal or a Man in a Suit. The voice itself had told her that resistance would be useless, that in the end she would give in, and then the catastrophe would occur, and destiny be fulfilled. Still she stood up to the voice and swore to herself in a frenzy of irritation that nothing would happen, while the voice assured her that it would, whether she liked it or not. And indeed it did, all the time: she only had to be absent-minded for a moment in the forest of problems which made up their life and – like the Day of Judgement – the Man in the Suit would come upon her unawares, naked, and make her tremble like Our Lady . . . and it would happen.

She was in no sense warped, or morally flawed, and her behaviour and way of life were unimpeachable. She was a nice country girl with a superior mind that was capable of some finesse; it was this that had led her to choose Hamid rather than Mustafa, although Mustafa was an official night-patrolman with a guaranteed wage, and he also had a tiny patch of land and a small buffalo of his own. Hamid meanwhile had not a penny in the world and was at least five years older than Mustafa, and was dark brown, almost black. But she would be doing her mind an injustice if she said that it was responsible for the choice: behind it there was always an obscure hazy finger pointing, which almost spoke to her, insisting, demanding that she should take Hamid rather than Mustafa, because Hamid was working in Cairo.

She had known all along that her life in their village was limited, and that inevitably, in one way or another, she would end up living in the capital. That vast shining place, 'The Mother of the World' they called it, that with its splendour and luxury peeled away the deposits left by squalor and abuse and transformed those who lived there into men and women of class. Hadn't her cousin Fatima who'd gone there to work as a maid come back looking like a European? You could hardly recognize her when she got off the train wearing a dress and carrying a handbag. So what about her, when she wasn't going to be a maid but the wife of the doorman of a block of flats high as the sky?

The voice that whispered to her and convinced her that her place was in Cairo had certainly turned out to be right. As everybody assured her, she was not made to work the hard earth from sunrise to sunset; her white body, pure white, was created for life in the capital and her prettiness was not of the countryside. For, by village standards, Fathiyya was pretty, one of the prettiest girls in her village, fair-skinned like a rich man's daughter – and only the rich are fair-skinned. It was true that she was tall and skinny, but that was the diet of oil and maize, and when she started to eat white bread and butter she would grow plumper. Her place was in Cairo, and strangely enough the voice which kept reiterating this notion to her did not come from outside her, but from within.

There she would live, where the streets were broad and sweet and clean and not a speck of dust would cling to you if you lay down to sleep on them. The great spread of shining flashing lights at night-time changed darkness into broad daylight, or something more wonderful than daylight. The women were beautiful and looked like Europeans, and the men had pink faces, and were rich and drove cars and spent pounds without a pang of regret as the money left their pockets. There was food in abundance, kebabs, sweet smells, hotels; and there the Nile, the mighty Nile, had its source.

In this paradise she would find her place; the hidden voice had always assured her of this and so she was not at all surprised when matters settled themselves. Hamid approached her, her family were hesitant and it was she who was full of enthusiasm and accepted him gladly.

Only a week later she set off and found herself at last, as she had dreamt she would be a thousand times, in the heart of Cairo, in the building whose ten storeys she had always tried to picture to herself. It must be said that she did not actually live on any one of the ten floors, but in Hamid's room, which had been hastily constructed for him under the stairs by the owner of the building as an incitement to whoever might marry him, for they hoped that in Hamid's wife, when he married, they would have a maid who would solve the problem of domestic help for them.

But the room was spacious in spite of everything, and it had a bed with a real mattress and a small cupboard and electric light.

It must be said too that Fathiyya, beautiful in their village, appeared strange in Cairo. To the inhabitants of the building she looked like a puppet, a bride puppet. She was certainly tall and fair-skinned, and her features were beautiful in a way: she had nice eyes, and a small pretty nose – impossible that it should be the nose of a peasant woman – and a delicate mouth like Solomon's ring, but the trouble was that they appeared quite unsuited to her build and size. It was as if the head of a small child had been mounted on a woman, or as if the head had somehow shrunk, and the body stayed the normal size.

But what mattered was that Hamid became light-hearted, changed from the surly, ferocious-looking creature who had snarled and shouted all day to a cheerful human being, busy as a bee, running up and down stairs, jumping up from his seat, greeting people, fetching and carrying, obeying orders. And Fathiyya meanwhile remained crouched in her place facing the door of the room observing the broad entrance and the great glass door of the block of flats, watching Cairo, or more exactly that portion of the street outside, which constituted Cairo in her eyes.

She crouched withdrawn, still knowing only what she had seen between the railway station and the block of flats, contemplating the dream become reality. Cairo, Cairo, much more magnificent than she had imagined or than her cousin had been able to describe, a thousand times grander and more wonderful. Could such crowds of people, such broad streets, such wide squares, really exist? Were people able to live in the midst of that dreadful crush of cars, that went so fast that they'd swallow you up if you were off your guard for a moment. The shops and the hoardings and the lights, all colours of the rainbow, flashing on and off, pulsating like single drumbeats through lines of music, the tumult, the uproar, the constant festivities. For it had seemed to her, when, after something of a struggle, Hamid had managed to drag her terrified, bewildered, half-mad, into the middle of the square before the railway station, that it must be some feast or saint's day or another celebration that she didn't know about, to make the people congregate in such vast numbers and make a noise that set her ears jangling. But Hamid had told her, laughing in a knowing way, 'It's like that every day'.

What a city, where people lived every day as if it were a saint's day or a feast.

Yet as she shrank behind the half-open door of the room, seeing from a distance now, and pondering, she began to notice in Cairo, condensed for her in the section of the street facing her, things that she would never for a moment have expected to find in the dream city. Poor people, properly poor, and hungry, and beggars; even in their village itself poverty did not exist in such extremes of ugliness. People lied and swore and were rude to each other, and there were thieves and pickpockets: theft made the existence of her husband and others like him necessary, and provided him with stories of incidents both in the neighbourhood and far away, that he would relate to her.

The Cairo ladies, whom she had imagined at first to be without exception women of taste, reaching European standards of fashion and beauty, she now realized numbered many ugly ones among them. The majority would have been ugly, had it not been for the red and white paint that they daubed on their faces, and this made them take on colour and shine like newly polished shoes and, she concluded eventually, left their owners even more ugly than they would have been without it. The abundance of these ugly women was such that she began to feel a sort of satisfaction with herself. In the beginning she had put her market value no higher than that of a maid to the least of them, but her self-esteem had risen to the point where she reckoned that if she had been dressed like them she would have become the centre of attention, and been considered a real beauty as she had been in the village.

Hamid himself seemed to have some sense of his own importance and pride in his job, although she quite failed to understand the nature of his work when they told her about it. She supposed that he had something of the status of official night-watchman in the village who carried a gun and commanded respect and fear, but from what she saw of him at work, he looked more like a servant: inclining his head to her, rushing to carry out the orders of Mrs So-and-So, being bellowed at and scolded by the owner of the building in unfamiliar phrases with words like 'dunce' and 'hypocrite', quite meaningless to Fathiyya, although she presumed that they were perhaps swear-words in Cairo.

Even so, she didn't like the attitude of lofty disdain which he adopted towards the owner of the building the day he tried to insist that Hamid let her work for them: Hamid refused outright, vowing that he himself would stop working for them if they tried to force her. It was a point of view that she couldn't accept when she thought of the pitiful way they lived, and their position in the scale of things, so low that it didn't allow them even the equanimity of spirit that comes from having five pounds to your name. This was an opportunity to have enough to live on and to buy a warm dress for winter, and it was more than likely that they would have been given a good meal from time to time. But Hamid refused, rash and capricious, and when she opened her mouth to argue with him he shouted at her, as if he owned the building and she was a tenant on the eighth floor.

The truth of the matter was that the economic justification for her desire to work was no more than a pretext, and what she really wanted was to get to know the people of Cairo better, to go into their homes and talk to them. Shut up in the room as she was, her shy introverted nature didn't allow her to do any such thing. Faced with the curious stares of the tenants who stormed the threshold, boring into her for a few moments as they scrutinized her appearance, the way she sat, her clothes, and then smiled or muttered vaguely or merely mocked, she became more closed in on herself and the chains tightened around her. They were chains of her own making; like the tenants of the building, the city around her was always on the move, surging forth, teeming with life, everything in it flowing along and coming together. But she to a certain extent, and her husband Hamid, were not only unable to abandon themselves to the city and its movement, to let it do with them what it did with the others, but were terrified and appalled by it, and recoiled more tightly in upon themselves.

She did, at least, but Hamid – and this dated exactly from the time he had married her and she had come to Cairo – had been able to free himself somewhat, moved about more easily, went to Sayyida Zaynab, to the suburbs, knew where you should change going to al-Husayn. It was not just where he went either, but his attitude of *savoir-faire*, his air of understanding what went on. He seemed to Fathiyya a different person from the dark silent shy youth from their village, who would turn his face away if he encountered a procession of women and girls carrying water jars early in the morning. Now he laughed and joked with the men at the garage, collected the rents and reckoned up the money to the last half penny, and even had friends who were natives of the city, not his relations or men from the same part of the country as him.

It was she alone who remained a prisoner in the room, bound by the narrow crack through which she saw the world of Cairo; and she sensed that the city was not a world, but a sea, shoreless and unfathomable. She was going along the brink, but if she once forgot and let her feet carry her on, that would be the end of her. What was frightening was that the sea was not tranquil and still, and did not adopt the same stance in relation to her as she to it; it was oppressive, a heavy sea, and thousands of hands stretched out from it, thousands of smiles beckoned from it, treacherous sirens calling to her, smoothing the way for her to plunge in.

Even the eager call of one of the tenants, with the money in his hand and the greengrocer's nearby, was a hand reaching out from the sea, paralyzing her with the terror of it and making her freeze where she stood. She withdrew further into herself until it was as if she had seen and heard nothing. She turned away covering her head, in flight, praying for a miracle to deliver her from the situation. Meanwhile the tenant, giving up, shot her a glance which she did not see, but she felt it, like a bullet in her head, and her ears picked up his muttered comments correctly interpreting the obscenities contained there.

She was shy, introverted, withdrawn: so be it, but life has its incontrovertible rules from which there is no escaping. With her first pregnancy Fathiyya had emerged from the room so that her world extended to include the entrance, and with her second child, which followed the first in a matter of months, it took in the pavement adjoining the building and the one opposite, then the street in both directions up to the square which opened out of it.

And now Fathiyya began to answer back, and even to initiate conversation. She ran errands and learnt to distinguish between the car bringing the doctor's son home from school and the one carrying the son of the man who worked for the radio. She knew all the gossip about the tenants from Hamid, and from others, and eventually it reached the point where she became Hamid's source of information about them and their affairs. The story of the midnight visitor who knocked at the flat of the airline employee, especially when he was on night duty at the airport, was only an intimation of what she came to know about the seamy side of life in Cairo, the scandals and intrigues that took place constantly beneath the respectable affluent surface. This is the exclusive province of the concierge, and still more of his wife, with her greater persistence and wiliness in these matters. Despite her narrowness of vision, she sees a lot especially in the night, and although her mind is small she can tell the difference between the sister of the man whose wife and children are spending the summer holidays in Alexandria, while he's up to his ears in work darling and simply can't get away, and his real sisters who visit the family throughout the year.

Oddly enough, none of this spoilt the dream in Fathiyya's head completely: she modified it, but she never lost sight of it. The great city remained great in her eyes, although she could see the bad things everywhere, and this was always her reply to Hamid when every now and then he came back cursing Cairo and everyone in it, having suffered this or that at the hands of one of its inhabitants.

If the ugly slime of evil lay at the bottom then salvation must lie in learning how to float. In this way Fathiyya learnt to do what the other thousands and millions of people crowded into Cairo did, floating as they floated in the great terrible surges of movement that rolled through the city.

The only things that ruffled the calm surface of her life sometimes were the tremors set up by the sudden emerging of the apparition which lay in wait for her and ambushed her in the thick of her many duties: the Man, naked, like a dreadful hand stretching out and threatening to pull her down into the mud and filth: and that voice assuring her that the end result of her being in Cairo would be to make her see that she was going to descend to forbidden territory with the Man and there was nothing she could do about it. These occasions left Fathiyya exploding with annoyance and irritation and disgust, and determined too that it should never happen, even if she paid with her life. Just you wait and I'll get even with you, Cairo.

In a big city full of wolves, daytime and night-time, in buses and cars, on the pavements, in queues, it would be inconceivable that a big block of flats should escape having one of its own.

If the truth were known it had more than one, but it would be absurd to concern ourselves with all of them, so let us be content with that particular good-looking, fair-skinned young man living in the single flat on the ground floor. Of all the people living in the building, he was the most charming and lively and modest, obliging and ready to help, and well-versed in treating others with the right measures of deference and intimacy. None of this, of course, implies that he was not a wolf, for this dazzling surface concealed worse than that – an evil hyena without honour or a sense of wrong.

He was obsessed with women, and would go to ridiculous

lengths to get hold of one. His idea of having a woman was to spend one night with her and then start looking for another, as if he were committed to working his way through them before his time ran out. He was thirty-five now and his reputation was untarnished, or rather it was a mark of his ingenuity that he had been able to hide his secret life from the society that he frequented, and could hold his head up in the company of honourable men, as what went on inside him was known only to his victims. And even they forgave him often, indeed some of them loved him and clung on to him, and then suffered horrible shocks from his torture of them.

Naturally he had run through everyone who had caught his eye in the flats. But then, he was coming in from work one day – and Hamid greeted him after the normal fashion of concierges which he had now perfected, so that he could make you imagine that he had stood up, while in fact he had never left his seat – and there was Fathiyya sitting in the doorway of their room offering her snow-white breast to the child in her arms; snow-white but skinny too, so skinny that any ordinary person on seeing it would not have been able to help but pity its owner.

But our wolf – the Man in the Suit – did not feel pity. He glanced at her, then, either intentionally or unintentionally, turned to look at Hamid who was again sitting with his thin legs stretched out in front of him, one crossed over the other. He played with a cheap rosary which had some beads missing, and his dark pitted face, whose scars bore witness to the smallpox that had visited him in his childhood, was again lit up by a good-natured smile, full of the naive joy of innocence. He looked as if, had he been accustomed to acting in such a way, he might have reprimanded his older child – with languid enthusiasm – for drawing on the marble of the entrance hall with a piece of chalk he'd come across in his play; but he was clearly content with the boy's masculine naughtiness and this made him turn from scolding him to asking Fathiyya playfully to give him a third son who might perhaps emerge calm and gentle like his mother.

All this the Man in the Suit took in in the short time needed to reach the door of his flat and put his key in the lock. Instantly his mind was fixed on a course of action in a way that was undoubtedly complex and odd. For while people might shake their heads or smile pityingly at such a scene the worst they would be likely to do, even if they were full of ill-will, would be to mock inwardly at this poor little happy family. But his immediate reaction was to decide without reservations to devour Fathiyya, and add her to his list of victims.

No ordinary wolf this then, but a hyena, drawn to his victims for the very reasons that would make others keep away. The times he'd been happiest sleeping with women were when he'd forced himself on a widow the same night her elderly husband had died, or when he'd had an affair with the mother of a fellow-student of his. Now there was this scared withdrawn creature whom he'd once addressed a few words to only to have her turn and flee; she of the white skinny breast, wife of the tall dark peasant Hamid. There was no cure for her introversion, for her fear of him and of Cairo and the people there; but perhaps if he went to her, and had her, then she would stop hiding away, and learn to associate with her fellows in the city.

His particular genius, for each person has his own special talents, was that no sooner had he taken a decision like this than his mind began to devise ways and means of realizing it; they were hellish ones, and it was inconceivable that a human mind was responsible for them. For he was torpid and idle, grudging even a smile, except on those occasions when his eye alighted on a woman and he made up his mind to have her. Within a second he was another person, pulsating with life, his mind erupting with plans and ideas, confronting life with such obvious zest that you would hardly know him.

Before he had turned his key in the lock his hand went up to his forehead in a feigned gesture of distress at his forgetfulness, his wallet came out and a five-pound note was held under Hamid's nose. 'A packet of Cleopatras, Hamid. I forgot to buy them. You get them for me will you. It doesn't matter how far you have to go or what price you have to pay. You'll have the five-pound note on you. Don't come back without them, Hamid, even if you have to go out into the suburbs.'

The cunning of it, as he flung the door to embezzlement wide open for Hamid, embezzlement on a limited scale, an enticement to stay away for longer than necessary, to make exaggerated claims for the tiresomeness of the task. And Hamid, ever good-hearted, swallowed the bait in an instant and decided, even before he had got up from his place, that he should make at least threepence out of the deal and it was up to him to show that he deserved it.

As for you, my shrinking violet ... having made sure that Hamid had left the building, he retraced his steps, opening the door of his flat, which was no more than a couple of paces from the door of the room under the stairs. 'May I have the pleasure ... Fathiyya? Really? So you're Fathiyya. And the baby? Sultan? What nice names. And this little boy? Antar? Well. A real family of heroes. And what about the other children? There aren't any more?'

That's a good start, my opening gambit: 'If I were Hamid there'd be another on the way.'

But with this the seasoned Don Juan only discovered that he seemed to be having little effect on Fathiyya. Either she was stupid or she was pretending to be. In either case he would have to change tack. Money? That sort didn't understand the value of money. Only someone who handled money and knew how to spend it understood its value. Love? They didn't contemplate falling in love, or certainly not with someone like him. They never looked further than the ends of their noses, and if they did happen to aspire to something a little higher than their own class it would never be to the dizzy heights of a good-looking professional man who treated a five-pound note with such lordly disdain. And so, my little duck of skin and bone, what's the best way to eat you all up? A long-term plan was needed: first of all he would have to make the scared creature have confidence in him and lose her fear, then move in gradually, drop his pose with her and seize the opportunity when it presented itself, or create it if necessary, and encircle her, so that she was forced to capitulate.

But scarcely had he begun to apply himself to the problem than he realized that, despite all his skill and practised sweet-talking, his intuition had failed him that time: as he started out to allay her fears, he could see that it was more like dealing with a snail than a human being. Whenever she picked up a sound or sensed a figure approaching, she drew herself in until she was transformed into a mute mass of flesh and bone incapable of transmitting or receiving information. Up till then he had not had a good look at her: he had seen her face only once and as soon as she had become aware that he was looking at her, she had covered it. So she had vanished from his sight although she was still there in front of him. His good looks were his most powerful weapon and he had wanted her to see him, sure that if she once looked at him, and studied his features for a while, something would happen to her, just as it had done to all her predecessors. But how would she ever see him when he felt all the time he was trying to talk to her that something inside her was preventing her from listening? Or if she was listening, she was not conscious of the meaning of what he said, and was unable to reply to him, or even to look and see who was talking to her.

Fathiyya could have been exposed inadvertently to this confrontation when she first came to live in the building, but now that she had been outside in the street and begun to have dealings with the people there and with the tenants themselves, it was up to the Man to carry it through by himself. Fathiyya would certainly never have got involved in it by chance, for she wasn't stupid and was never off her guard. When their first brief innocent conversation was followed by another, which she felt to be contrived and artificial, all her old fears about Cairo and the sea and the hands stretching out to her were suddenly re-awakened. Terror filled her at the thought of the Man in the Suit whom the voice had often intimated to her; not that it had given precise details about his appearance, but here certainly was a man in a suit, and she sensed that he had approached her on purpose. Was not this enough to make her feel that she was in the teeth of danger and that if she let slip one word or yielded an inch to him she would be lost, and the scene complete?

So excessive was her caution that she could scarcely sleep at night, and even the presence of Hamid himself did not reassure her, nor by locking the door and checking it and double-checking did she succeed in stifling her fears. Most unluckily for her, the voice had insisted that the event which it hinted at to her in whispers would happen, with or without her consent. She seemed to feel herself going mad but determined that, come what may, she would resist and on no account allow any connection to be established, any word to be exchanged, between her and this Man. The battle would rage within her in awful silence, unknown to any living creature, and she would never be able to divulge her secret.

It is easily possible to picture the extent and nature of the misfortune which afflicted our wolf-hyena when he saw his good looks, his skill, all his efforts expended in vain against the might of this fair-skinned peasant woman who recoiled and closed herself up to him. Now what had promised to be a simple brief affair had brought instead terror of defeat, and his self-confidence was so utterly shaken, that he felt compelled now not to embark on an affair but merely to prove to himself that he was still irresistible to women and couldn't fail with them.

The days flashed by at a bewildering speed until two months had passed since the time of his original decision and he was not a step nearer achieving it. He thought about his undertaking, and Fathiyya herself, day and night, until the whole subject was preoccupying him more than anything else in his life at the time, almost to the exclusion of all else. Sometimes he came to his senses and felt disgusted with himself at being in this state – he who had roamed the earth, sky and stars of the kingdom of womankind and tried them all from princesses to washerwomen, even beggars, that he should bestow so much time and effort and thought on a woman like Fathiyya. There was something wrong here which he couldn't work out, yet it was unthinkable that he should fail, and he would risk all to avoid it.

Sometimes he awoke to a question which he had never had to face before: could it be that he had fallen in love with Fathiyya? If love is gauged by the amount of time spent thinking about the beloved then his was a rare and powerful love – for it had never happened before that a man had devoted so much time to thinking about a woman as he did about Fathiyya. There he was: when he found that Fathiyya's rejection of him was complete and final, not the whimsical reaction of a particular moment or day, when he despaired completely of all his attempts, his one concern and hope became not to talk to her, not even to dream that he would make her give in, but just to see her. Nothing more than that, and yet even this simple demand, modest in the extreme, proved difficult to realize. Fathiyya's fear, and accordingly her cautiousness, had increased to the point where she hardly ever left the room, and when she was obliged to, she would rush back in terror as if a swarm of crocodiles were after her. If he wanted to see her the Man had to trust that chance would arrange matters for him, and to increase the possibilities of this he had to pass his time in the doorway of the building or in the entrance hall, or near the door of his flat. If he did that when Hamid was there it would inevitably invite suspicion, so he was forced to send him on errands. But to ensure that this did not provoke doubts in turn and that his pretext was always respectable and reasonable he had to be careful not to do it too often, and consequently this reduced the number of occasions when it was feasible for him to be near the door of their room. Just to see her was a complicated exercise consuming long days of time and effort. And even then he didn't really see her, but caught a glimpse of her, something black, the gallabiyya which she had reverted to for protection long after she had discarded it and dressed like the people of Cairo in colours and patterns.

It was noon on that summer's day, at the very hottest time, the time for siesta. He had waited the entire week for an opportunity to send Hamid off into the suburbs, and love and emotion and nervous tension had taken such a powerful hold on him that he couldn't stand a second more of it. He was at the end of his tether, and prepared to do anything to win even one word from her: tell her he loved her, offer to marry her, marry her at once, kill her if she refused, kill Hamid if he objected. He had descended to a state of such utter crushing despair that the only way left open to him was to storm the room and take it from there.

Because the older child had opened the door which his mother had locked and gone out into the side alley to play, he had only had to push the door and it had opened, and he had found himself face to face with her. She was standing at the head of the bed holding the baby. Although his head was so full of her and she had preoccupied him for so long and he had taken so many decisions relating to her, although there were the words that he had had ready to hurl down on her and beleaguer her with, at the sight of her, everything in his mind evaporated.

For Fathiyya it was as if the shades themselves, or death incarnate, had appeared to her; it was evil in a more determined form than anything she had conceived of hitherto. She had come

to place complete trust in all the measures which she had adopted
to be safe from him. Gradually she had begun to feel confident
that she had triumphed over the voice and over fate; it would be
ridiculous still to expect the dreaded event to take place now that
she had hedged herself in with so many precautions that it would
be impossible for that Man in the Suit to as much as see her.
Then to turn round suddenly to find him there in front of her, in
the empty room, with Hamid miles away, gave her the sensation
that she had unexpectedly lost her footing and tumbled from her
safe high place, and was plunging down into the bowels of the
earth, into the pit.

To realize that her will had been defeated by that of the voice,
and that there was the Man in the Suit appearing before her like a
figure of destiny, like a flesh and blood embodiment of the siren,
was to have a thunderbolt descending on her, and stupefying her.
She was not frightened as she stood there, simply dumbfounded
and paralyzed, having come to the end of her resources. In a flash
her fairness turned to greyish pallor, the grey yellowness of death.
She was deaf and her tongue swelled up and blocked her throat
and her links with life were severed by the stunning shock.

A sort of death struck her as it was to strike Hamid when he
saw her, and it was only an involuntary instinct for survival that
led her to reach out her hand, which had begun to tremble
noticeably in a way that was horrifying to see, and cling on to the
bedhead. The child at her breast began to slide down and, again
instinctively, she saved him from a sudden fall and he reached the
ground safely, sobbing loudly.

Once she was sure that her child was safe, there was no longer
any value in hanging on to life. Her body tottered and swayed
and threatened to fall, and fell. But it did not complete its fall
because immediately our hyena-wolf was there with both hands
ready to receive it. His mouth had dropped open in astonishment,
for the last thing he had been expecting was that the fruit would
fall of its own accord so easily into his hands. No words had been
necessary, no action, he had expended not the slightest effort. He
had come intending to fight the definitive battle with all his
resources, to take on not only Fathiyya or Hamid, but the world,
oblivious to the risks involved, of humiliation or imprisonment or
death.

He had despaired completely of making any gains, for it was hardly reasonable to suppose that she who begrudged him so much as a touch or a look would grant him any more than just that, a chance to see her even if the price was disgrace or violent death. And now, here she was, his to do what he wanted with, a fresh blossom, submissive as an abandoned scrap of clothing, giving him the chance to have all he could possibly dream of from her. She was more like a corpse and the resemblance only served to arouse the old hyena in him, and make his saliva run – the hyena that had disappeared into the depths of the person whom love and passion for Fathiyya had elevated to the ranks of the great lovers. In his frenzy he had experienced sleepless nights and jealousy and doubt and torment that enervated him, that weakened his body so he grew lean and emaciated, and that refined his feelings until he began to feel and think and behave like a poet. The hyena, who had almost suffocated and died, shook off the layers of unfamiliar sensations deposited on top of him and arose, a glint of triumph in his eyes. His body quivered in anticipation of the delights which surely awaited him and although he would have had only a moment to wait, he mustered his reserves of greed to obviate even that, to fall upon her and devour her straight away.

Seizing the opportunity offered by her passing loss of consciousness he laid her down and pushed the child viciously away. He began to shriek in high-pitched terror which activity the Man did not deny him, even relishing it for the spice which it added to the dish. With a practised unfeeling arm he embraced her, and with a hand scarcely believing in its own existence and its sudden overwhelming victory, he pushed down his trousers and ripped her clothes with a feeling of intoxication unlike any other on this earth. At this, even if she had been dying a real death, she would have been roused from her coma, for other instincts are controlled by that fundamental urge to have authority over our own bodies.

So it happened that while his excitement was steadily mounting, she came to her senses as if touched by an electric current. Although this awakening came only to her mind, she struggled to summon the feeble reserves of strength held by her body to articulate its final refusal, and resisted. She moved uneasily, a form of opposition which only served to call into operation the concealed power of the wolf-hyena, and his arms and legs encircled her, unrelenting chains of steel. She squirmed, he covered her, both exerting themselves to the full. She could have shouted for help and enlisted other people in her struggle, but she refused, because the fight was hers alone. In any event the intervention of other people would only shame her now that the die was cast, and destiny fulfilled. They may have stood in the path of destiny, but they would also have been witnesses to its fulfilling, and it was in the disastrous nature of the affair that she was to defy a kind of death, a private fall, that no one else knew about, or faced with her.

The terror had gone from her and anger taken its place when she opened her eyes to examine her conqueror. A few inches away from her face, she saw his for the first time and her eyes widened in astonishment and resentment and fear, for she had never seen anything like it. It was a clean-shaven face, pink-cheeked and handsome, green eyes with long lashes, sweet breath, white even teeth, a beautiful mouth that any woman's mouth would feel like kissing. It wore a broad smile of triumph and pleasure that revealed profound dimples at either side and a beauty spot. She had often dreamt about this smile, as she had dreamt of the outstretched hands inviting her gently but insistently to leave the safety of land and plunge in and sink down to the shadows and slime.

When she saw the smile, she resisted with fresh vigour as if it were the slimy depths trying to entice her with soft cunning. Her struggling only made it easier for him to entwine his limbs more tightly around hers so that they seemed to be touching at every point. She had persisted in her fear of the evil until it had appeared to her, and of the voice's whispered warnings until they had materialized. Her determination and prudence had never left her until the dice was thrown and the prohibition violated. Then it was all over with her, and the continual fear and the whisperings of the voice and the dream and the reality fused in a strange crowded moment, so abundant with sensation that it would have filled many such moments, but what predominated in it was the realization that it was no longer any use to be afraid or to resist.

All that was left to her was to throw herself on his mercy, to adopt the stratagems of those without power, and weep, and cringe: 'I'm at your mercy. I've got small children who need me'.

Her words and her tears only added just the right zest to the meal for the old hyena, and when she continued to sob more bitterly, it was not from a desire to intensify her pleading with him. For now she was crying with real feeling, from the depths of her soul, for herself and her helplessness. But these tears, surprisingly enough, did not go on for long.

She had begun to experience strange feelings that transmitted new surprising things to her, assailing her like the flash and glitter of Cairo had done. She saw a carnival of light and colour, red, blue and violet neon. Smooth handsome faces, elegant clothes swam before her eyes, perfumes that aroused and lulled her, wide avenues thronged with life, clean healthy mothers and children, and parks, and trees; trees that even had their leaves clipped and shorn like coiffeured ladies. Trains and fast cars roared towards her and people poured out of cinemas and cabarets and dancing places, all the city coming together and flowing into her. And she trembled, defeated and bewildered. But despite her impotence and her recognition of her crushing defeat, still she resisted and the strange sensations kept on coming. She took on the city single-handed but it penetrated the secret hidden parts of her, careless of her opposition.

It was inevitable that in the end she should abandon her attempts at opposition out of tiredness and despair, convinced that it was all in vain and that no miracle would save her at the last minute. It had all happened just as the voice had predicted and her will had no part to play. But what the voice had not mentioned, and what she would not have imagined possible, was that the submission imposed on her by defeat began to change into submission born of enjoyment, and that was something which, even while it was happening, she couldn't believe. Scarcely had she started to feel it when the door had opened and there in the doorway stood Hamid, tall and thin and dark as dark, looking as if he'd seen a ghost.

Hamid continued to stand by the door, which he had unconsciously closed behind him. Fathiyya was still on the ground clinging to the bedhead, her legs apart but her body covered, one desire lodged in her mind, unmoving, that Hamid would do what he had to do quickly. For it was the only way and fate would surely offer it to him. How could life go on after all that had happened? Nothing could go back to being as it was, things couldn't be put right, and it was ridiculous to suppose that either of them would find peace of mind unless she died, and he was the one who killed her. Yet the strange thing was that whenever the voice had reached this point it had said quite unequivocally that Hamid wouldn't kill her and that some other destiny awaited her.

Hamid tired of standing looking for so long and sat down. The older child rushed in from outside noisily demanding food, and when he felt the charged unbroken silence fear gripped him. He grew quiet and was soon asleep; darkness fell outside and the gloom in the room became absolute and all-embracing.

Nobody dared to switch on the light.

Hamid stayed sitting by the door moking from the small packet of cigarettes that he'd bought with what he'd put by from the Man in the Suit's money. With immense calm Fathiyya sat up, then lay down, then sat up again, waiting for Hamid to do it and be finished. All she secretly hoped from him was that he would not catch her unawares, but that somehow he would take pity on her and give her some warning; she had had enough surprises and there was not a spark of resistance left in her to withstand another.

She tried to speak and he silenced her with a growl like a wounded animal.

She drifted off for a second and woke to the sound of a man's low stifled sob. Her senses reeled, not trusting the evidence before them. Would he have done that if they'd been in their village? The curse had got him as well, Cairo had defeated him, made him soft, sapped his will so that he was no longer capable of killing his wife when he'd caught her in the act. Could it be true that he was weeping for her lapse?

She would have crawled towards him begging him to stop crying like a woman, to be a man again and put her out of her misery. She would have, but when she opened her mouth to plead, a shout like the roar of an angry lion rose up, and she was transfixed where she lay.

Hamid didn't kill her but at dawn the little family left through

the great dreadful door of the building. Hamid carried all their
belongings rolled up in a yellowed sheet and slung over his
shoulder on the end of his heavy stick. With his free hand he
dragged the older child along, half-asleep. Fathiyya, in front,
carried the other child. Although she didn't know where they
were going her only fear for the moment was that the boy would
catch cold and she lifted up the skirt of her robe and began
winding it tightly round him to protect him. Mutely she urged
Hamid to take a blanket from the roll and wrap it around the
older child, but the words never left her mouth for they had not
spoken to each other since the day before.

The little caravan went on its way protected from the early
morning cold by high walls. The shadows of one building relinq-
uished them only to yield them up to the shadows of another, for
the moon-like sun of dawn had risen. The caravan withdrew furtively from the big city which slept on in silence careless of them
and the horrors which weighed upon them, snoring innocently, at
peace with itself as if it had done nothing. Hamid's anger
mounted until he could have hurled his bundle aside and lashed
out with his stick, shattering the lighted shop windows and the
gleaming cars tucked away for the night, and the washed asphalt
of the streets. With all his heart he had begun to loathe the very
act of walking on those streets even when it was to get out of the
city which had become for him a suffocating nightmare.

He bought tickets for them on the next train, but he went back
to their village without Fathiyya. In the crowds coming and going
around the main railway station she slipped away from him back
into Cairo of her own free will this time, not in response to any
siren's call.

Rings of Burnished Brass
A story in four squares

(((((())))))

The first square

Her back had become a mass of squares, searing, red-hot, little ones inside big ones, full of pain. She should be gentle and think clearly, be tender. But she had never wanted it to be like this, didn't want it now; she must cry out and push him away with all harshness.

'What are you doing? Stop it. Stop it.'

An unexpected development, and she assumed he would react wildly and terrorize her into submission. But, lying half on his side with his leg bent up and his hand hovering, uncertain what to do next, he was silent. His eyes were wide open in astonishment, and his features were those of a child who has done wrong in spite of himself, and wants to be good.

'What's the matter?'

He was scared to come near her, or touch her. She didn't answer. What could she say? How could she make him understand things which she herself, even though she felt them, didn't know how to shape within the limits of comprehensible words. Was this the time to retreat, to make the final renunciation? But how could she, when what she had envisaged as the most abhorrent, the most preposterous turn of events had already come to pass?

Consumed with rage and despair, she felt a hand, like a cat sneaking up to take what it knew it shouldn't have. She pushed it aside with a strength and lack of pity that she hadn't intended, uncharacteristic of her and unfamiliar.

There was silence, so dense that the harsh rattle of the street, the light-hearted cries of playing children, the hum of life outside, was swallowed up. Would Sayyida Zaynab* punish her? She

---

* Granddaughter of the Prophet. Patron saint of women and the infirm with a mosque containing her shrine in Cairo. *Sayyida*: 'lady'.

shuddered. Was she losing her mind? Should she scream, or run out, as if there was something to escape from, and tell everybody? Or simply kill herself?

Her mind gave way to distraught meanderings, and before she could think of anything else she glanced sideways at him, imperceptibly, barely moving her eyes in their sockets, and then stopped abruptly: without a sound, without any gathering of pressure, or any concentration of energy on his part or even a shift of position, tears made their way slowly from between his closed eyelids and left their tracks gleaming on his cheeks. And so once again, she was caught up in a rush of feeling like a whirlwind, that made her forget everything and go to him impatiently, embrace him with arms that froze with longing, rain down anxious kisses upon him, summon all her energy to keep him from being hurt, bathing his cheeks and his eyelids with her tongue and, in her excess of desire, delighting in the taste of his tears. *[handwritten: this is end of third sequence]*

She was finished. Suppose it was his fault, then so be it. She would sooner die than see him weep again, and it was her fate, or her bad luck, all determined in advance – the crowd at the door of Sayyida Zaynab, the push from behind when her foot was poised in mid-air. She had been quite certain that nothing could stop her from falling and her only hope had been that she would not crack her head on the big square tiles. But the arrangement was perfect. As she went down, bound for certain disaster, a hand came out to save her. It seemed not to belong to anyone, as if it were a hand from the skies, but it prevented her falling any further. Then as she lost her balance in the process of recovery an arm went round her, sturdy and capable, and for a split second it made her feel, perhaps for the first time since before her husband had died, quite safe.

So she hadn't fallen, and no bones were broken. But Sayyida, Mother of Hashim, Mother of the Helpless, I did you wrong. Forgive me. Her bag. There was the other hand holding it out. And only then did she begin to realize that the arm was still around her. She expressed her thanks, backing away in the confusion of extricating herself from a predetermined fate. What did he say? She didn't know. In the end she had looked into his face, and the shock of it: he was hardly old enough to shave, and all the time she had assumed that she was dealing with a man.

'Why are you crying? Have I done something? Is it me that's upset you?'

'You pushed me away.'

'And that's what upset you!'

'You did it violently, as if you hated me. And you do, you despise me. You want someone rich, and respected. And I'm poor, and the poor don't have feelings as far as people like you are concerned.'

And in spite of himself, or perhaps because he chose to, he burst into tears. She took him in her arms. He didn't understand, it was ridiculous to expect him to. She possessed no faculties which made her capable of expressing to him the feeling that nothing mattered except that she had found him, and at that moment he was dearer to her than the whole world.

'What shall I do to make you believe me?'

'Don't push me away.'

'But I'm old enough to be your mother.'

'She died ten years ago. I haven't got a mother, you know that.'

He tried to speak but the tears choked him. He wanted to tell her how he felt like the abandoned castle in the story when life began to stir in it again. It had happened when he first put his arm round her and she felt not flabby and fat but ladylike and delicate and so soft that you could feel it even through the black silky layers of her clothes. He could have accepted her thanks and gone but he stood there, hesitating, wishing for a moment that she would need him again.

The next step was not arranged by fate. It was true that she had twisted her foot, but she would have been quite able to bear the slight pain and proceed alone. Why then, when she tried to walk, did she exaggerate her suffering and the extent of her injury? Was it because she had noticed that he wavered and that, strange as it may have seemed, he appeared to want her to want him?

With neither a word of objection nor a sign of acceptance from her he walked along beside her supporting her under her arm with a gentleness and tenderness that she had long since forgotten, like that of sons before they become men and transfer their affections to their wives and lovers.

Their stately progress might have been expected to end at the
first bus or tram stop or the sighting of a taxi but they continued
walking. She didn't request it and he didn't inquire. No conversation passed between them except when from time to time she
asked him, 'Am I tiring you?' and he denied it each time with
mounting scorn.

'What shall I do to convince you that you're very dear to me?'

'Don't push me off.'

'But I could be your mother. It's not right.'

She was always taking refuge in that, but the way she said
'your mother' was as if she didn't want him to believe in it. With
her death his own mother had deprived him of herself and of all
female company. Now she, this 'lady', was giving it back to him
all at once and he felt as if he were dreaming, and discovering his
hunger and loss for the first time. When he'd supported her, the
pressure of her comfortable affectionate body had almost driven
him wild, and he had visions of her adopting him as the son she'd
always wanted and leaning on him every day with this comfortable familiarity. But then his arm had appeared to begin to take
on a life of its own, far removed from any of his thoughts about
her. The body which it encircled seemed to melt, luxuriously, and
in spite of himself his arm, with its torn overalls hanging off it,
participated, and transmitted to him through all her clothes –
expensive but much too warm for the time of year – that feeling of
softness. The only maternal characteristic left in her then was the
trembling softness common to serene well-covered, well-satisfied
women who remain feminine well into their sixties, although she
didn't look even fifty. In his mind he compared her favourably
with the wife of their neighbour the taxi-driver, who after seven
years of married life looked as if all the things that had identified
her as a woman had withered away.

'Are you tired?'

'A little.'

'It'll be better like this.'

And he supported her with his whole arm so that it encircled
her. Now they had come into the area where he lived and she
began to learn about him: that he was eighteen, that he worked
with his father mending calor gas stoves, was an only child, and
that his mother had died during an operation. She had also begun
to understand why Sayyida Zaynab was angry with her.

This was not the first time she had gone to her, under protest, and the way there had been long. She had become a grandmother for the fourth time, and mother of a brilliant young company director, a university lecturer with a doctorate, tipped to become a government minister, a used car dealer, the richest of them all, and a daughter who was married and worked abroad.

Her contentment was justified, and need know no bounds. She had done her duty with consummate success, although her late husband had died along the way. People acclaimed her as an exemplary mother, and her children came to visit her at every religious festival and on every special occasion. You're looking well. You will come, won't you? What have you been doing with yourself? But they were only words.

Three men and a woman who didn't need her any more. They talked indulgently to her and teased her gently, and began to make fun of the old things in the flat that had accumulated over the years. Things that they had accorded love, even veneration, while they were growing up. Certainly there were still many ties that bound them so that she was anxious when she learnt that one of them was ill, and they in turn expressed concern for her blood pressure and her diabetes, but it was altogether different from the days when they were her children and she was really their mother. Theirs was the concern we feel for an old toy, when we hold it close and try to burrow into it, hoping to find just one jot of the comfort that it used to offer us; and she was as happy as them if she could give them what they wanted, solace perhaps in the face of that larger society where they now lived their lives, even though a gulf of many years separated them from those early days – except at Friday dinner-times.

From the early morning, she slaved with her old servant to make for each of them what he or she liked best. And in a tumult of noise and gaiety they began to arrive. There was the son whom she would still remind you used to be so pale and skinny when he was a child, grown into a husband; a husband of some long standing with sons and daughters who called her 'Tante', and 'Granny', and 'Grandma'. Her boy had become a whole separate family, and had secrets of his own, and whispered and made signs to his wife or to another brother. Only she was excluded from the game, and stood apart.

The food was brought, and they ate. And although deep inside

her she had long ago realized that it would have been better for all
of them if her cooking had remained a sweet memory, growing
more pleasurable with the passing of time, the present reality,
staring her in the face, was that they had quite lost their taste for
it, and swallowed it with difficulty. For their wives had given
them other food, such things as it would never have occurred to
the mother to think of preparing, and the meal and their
exaggerated approving comments had become a worn-out ritual
that she could hardly stomach, as indeed had the whole business
of their Friday visits to her.

Her children came to watch their own children hugging the old
grandmother, and then amused themselves by making them
practise saying her name; and perhaps the occasion aroused a
faint childhood memory here and there. It was a charade, and
when the players tired of it they would retire, each one in a corner
with his wife, or in a group discussing something of no relevance
to her. Then from time to time, perhaps at the jolt of a slow-
reacting conscience, one of them would lean across towards her
with a word, a compliment, or a perfunctory kiss, and it would
dawn on her that, although she was in her own home, making
them welcome, giving them food, she was an encumbrance that
they would feel compelled to cast off before long. And sure
enough the chain of discoveries would begin.

One would look at his watch and draw his breath in sharply: 'I
forgot. I've got a lecture.'

And the distress of the minutes or hours which she spent with
the rest of them, discomfited by her awareness that each one of
them must be searching for an original idea, a respectable excuse,
that he might use in order to get away himself. Even the children
tired of listening to her telling stories and asked to have the televi-
sion on, and in desperation she would go to the kitchen sometimes, to take refuge with the servants, only to find them
immersed in gossip about their ladies and gentlemen and the
neighbours, and the latest weddings and divorces among singers
and film stars. In the end after all the dreadful noise and uproar
she was alone again in the vast high-ceilinged flat. Even the old
servant had taken the afternoon off.

It was nobody's fault. Life was like that, and her children only
needed her as a decorative appendage, mother embalmed in the

'family' flat. When her husband had died she hadn't thought for a moment of remarrying or changing her style of life for they were there, her children, not allowing her out of their sight for a moment, so great was their need for her. And she in turn would not let herself be apart from them for long, for she wanted them always to be able to take from the waters of the verdant spring that flowed within her; her greatest happiness was to give herself to them, although it was only natural that the day would come when they no longer needed her. But what was she supposed to do when the mother in her lived on, potent and unsubdued, for she had married and had had children while still young?

'For heaven's sake, why not visit the Sayyida?'

Like a miracle from on high the suggestion came to deliver them from their difficulty, these sons who would enjoin despair and old age on their mother. They wanted her dumb, incapable, passive, dead above the earth's surface in readiness for the time when she should be transported to its depths, as if to erase from their minds the living articulate reality. She wasn't an old woman yet, even if she wasn't as young as she had been when their father died, and old age was something she would resist with all her might, in the near future at least. They wished it on her in part to justify to themselves her being alone, for a life of solitude is taboo for a young girl or a woman in her prime, but acceptable for an old woman. And so the suggestion that she should visit the Sayyida seemed like an answer to prayer.

Have mercy on us, Sayyida.

On Fridays, after the family lunch when she had had the enjoyment of seeing them ranged side by side around the lavish board, the men with their children, the daughter with her husband, and had dandled the grandchildren in turn on her lap, she was to go to the Sayyida and spend the rest of the day at her devotions.

And next year, God willing, you'll go on the pilgrimage to Mecca, and we'll rely on you to pray for us dearest mother, and don't forget to pray that Muna will be successful and Hamada will get his degree, and that the chairman of the board will resign and leave the way clear for me.

'What do you think about it, mother?'

And they all turned to the youngest brother who had begun to look as if he had found the buried treasure: the Sayyida every

Friday, and if you get bored, you can always go to Saint Al-Husayn on Mondays, and Saint Hanafy on Thursdays if you like. We're ready to help.

O yes, they were always ready to translate warmth of feeling, courteous attentions and filial duty into their cash equivalents, perhaps because they had begun to have money, while they no longer needed sympathy and demonstrations of affection.

Her fall was obviously devised by the Sayyida to show her anger, for she had never gone to her on her own initiative: she had been pushed by others, not into pious devotion, but towards a fate which she was powerless to stave off.

'We've walked a long way. I'm rather late. Shall we look for a taxi?'

'Are you fed up?'

She stared curiously at him. On his childish features the first vestiges of manhood were visible, giving him that particular beauty common to his age, a radiance which shines out irrespective of individual attributes. He had shaved his moustache, although you could almost count the roots of the shaven hairs one by one. His beard crept hesitantly down the sides of his face only to burst forth triumphantly like a fountain right in the middle of his chin, around and within a dimple. The look in his eyes was not insolent like a man's might have been, nor was the scope of his vision yet subject to the strictures of his will and his defining and limiting awareness. Yet he did not have the impudence of a child, rather the look of somebody who has begun to recognize the existence of other people, and as he looked at them, they were able to look back at him unobstructed. Her eyes had never met with such an entreaty before as, perhaps against his will, he seemed to beg her not to go. There was a world of difference between that and the doctor of philosophy or the company director saying to her, as they closed the door behind her at the end of one of her visits:

'Please . . . please, Mummy, stay and have supper with us.'

'Do you want to go? Won't you rest for a bit. To give the pain a chance to ease off.'

She gazed again at the insistent appeal in his eyes, and couldn't withstand it. It embarrassed her, for he didn't confirm his insistence with words, but left her to make the decision, and bring all her desire to stay into operation to crush her resistance to the idea. And so she asked: 'I really am tired, but where can I rest? I'll have to go.'

But with native cunning, he proposed an alternative. His father was in the shop. Their home was only a few steps away. It had a small sitting-room and one other room. Did she think it would be suitable?

Was he so naive that he didn't realize that anywhere would be suitable since she had received his urgent summons, and that it was what she most wanted to do, to make him happy, as far as it was in her power to do so, and that a wild spirit was surging through her making her capable of anything. She had ignored it always before, and tried to kill it, and her children had ignored it, and everyone around her had preached their values and received wisdom at her in an attempt to stifle it till it died of hunger and neglect and deprivation. But now that it had raised its head so violently it seemed to whirl her along on a magic carpet to a land of youth, vibrant, rumbling and pulsating with the movement of life, in its depths and its heights and on the surface of it: a land of sheer terror.

The look was not all need: at the heart of it there was desire silently burning, like a noiseless howl. But even if there was hell itself there, she, with her will, undertook to extract what she wanted from his look and compel it to give up the rest. He was a child, nothing more than a child, although he was taller than her, and was looking down at her, as if trying to steal a glance at himself through her eyes and see the things that weren't childish in him, the things that a woman might secretly want to take from him.

It was a risk and so she had to feel confident that her view of things would prevail – that she would give him a mother, even if only for a few hours, and that, perhaps unwittingly and very briefly, he would be a son to her; and that in any case she could no longer run away from what was to come.

It was strange, since his arm was still round her supporting her, and in Hanafy Street there were many eyes with little else to do but stare in search of a moment's excitement, strange, that they did not look with disapproval. Even the neighbours assumed she was a rich aunt dutifully seeking out her poor relations. So used were they to accepting all that they were subjected to that they wouldn't even have had any doubts when, as they got near to the top of the stairs leading to the flat, the hand supporting her moved down a little, feeling her back, and growing bolder.

She didn't want any time to be lost in feeling uncomfortable with him, so she made him understand, gently, that she had come with him not to rest, but because he had aroused maternal feelings in her. And it was only natural that she should tell a lie at this point and explain that this was because he reminded her of her own son whom she had lost when he was about the same age. He was motherless, and she was a mother whose children no longer aroused her maternal feelings or had any need of them. So she would be his mother for a little while but if any misunderstanding arose she would leave without further ado.

Of course he showed horror, and reassured her, and accepted her conditions, sure that she meant what she said, and deciding to himself that he would comply and enjoy her mothering him at first and then perhaps if he was lucky get the woman afterwards.

'You mean I'm like your son now?'

'And I'm your mother.'

'It's a nice idea . . . right, what are we going to do then?'

'What mothers do.'

She took off her outdoor clothes and, as water swilled over the floor that hadn't been cleaned for years, bent down with zeal, in spite of the pain, to polish and clean, while he went in and out noisily singing, happy. She sent him out with a basket and money and he came back with meat and vegetables, and soon the smell of cooking rose up. As the old gas stove slowly cooked the food in the clean orderly room, she went to the bathroom and washed everything she could lay her hands on, including his overalls, so that he sat there in some old clothes she had found for him, a little boy still.

With the washing nearly done, and the smell of food that was ready to eat, and his singing, grown more lusty now, and interspersed with little involuntary chuckles, she felt a happiness such as she had never known before, perhaps not even on her honeymoon. She hadn't married a sweetheart but – as people used to do in those days – an eligible man introduced to the family by a relation; and had it not been for the long cohabiting, the child-bearing, and her sweet disposition, she would have hated him, or who knows, perhaps she would have loved him, at least felt passionate sometimes, unsettled and changeable, instead of that everlasting sameness never soaring upwards and never sinking to the depths.

He had not known happiness like it even when his own mother was alive: for all her long suffocating kisses, she had never spoken to him without swearing at him, and when she took him in her arms his tender feelings were wounded by the thorniness of her rough affection. She had tried to temper it, be more motherly and gentle, but her insensitivity, her coarseness, had always reasserted itself. Now he could hardly remember her, or how he felt about her. All that had gone before was subsumed in his present happiness as, impetuously rushing here and there, laughing, teasing, he was alive as never before. Just as she had expected, her mothering had made him a child again, and this had restored touches of brightness to her that had long since faded, as if she'd just given birth for the first time.

Childishly he lifted the lid of the pot tasting scalding pieces of partly cooked meat, and she reproved him, then told him, in no uncertain terms, that everything in the flat was clean except him, and he was to have a bath, before the meal too. How he relished the situation as he tried to put off the torture till after lunch and she insisted in that deceptively soft way, that you realize belatedly is more intransigent than any abuse.

'Are you going to bath me then? You're my mother aren't you?'

He knew that he would be refused – he wasn't a baby, but perhaps he did it to find out just how far she would go, to what extent she had become the mother, and at what point she would recoil for shame. She pushed him in the direction of the bathroom, but he did not sense great disapproval. She was absorbed in the game, and what lay behind it was shrouded in obscurity.

'Scrub my back for me. Nobody's done that for me since my mother died.'

Even had she been gifted with extraordinary powers of insight, nothing would have made her understand why she accepted. She shouted at him to sit cross-legged with his back to the door; the loofah was eaten away and she couldn't help her hand coming into contact with his back. The muscles were firmer and harder than she had expected, and this made the heap of living flesh inclining towards her somehow unknown and fraught with danger.

She asked him if he'd scrubbed behind his ears with the loofah, only to discover, after a string of such questions, that he hadn't yet learnt how to bathe himself. Not only had he been deprived of a mother when he was young, but also of love, of a heart full of tenderness for him, of someone to insist that he ate, that he was clean and wholesome: he had been orphaned a thousand times over.

When she had finished and he was squirming to avoid the water pouring over him she had a sudden shock. His genitalia were visible to her for a moment and all at once there could be no more deceiving herself. For hours she had had an image of herself with a beloved son whom she'd come upon by chance, but this slender youth with the manliness that was in him was never he. He was a stranger born of quite another woman, and he had a father whom she had never seen, and a long life before seeing her of which she had only a shred of knowledge.

It was a momentary revelation but he realized, and understood, and was as confused as she was. All was changed when the spontaneous currents of motherly and filial feeling had been severed by a passing glance, and they had to take up their roles deliberately, with embarrassment, and the dreadful participation of the will. The bath ended suddenly, faded out by tacit consent, as if it was the cause of the tragedy.

Strange, after that confused medley of feelings, that, like a random spark, a small feeling of happiness came to her, as it might have come to any mother discovering one day that her son was no longer a child. The question that hung unresolved, as evening gathered in his father's shop, was one that she had not liked to articulate, but the answer came unsolicited: the father would be in a café with friends, smoking till after midnight, straining at a spluttering narghile, spluttering in turn and then relapsing into longer bouts of coughing. Similarly unsolicited came her reply that all that awaited her were the great high walls of the empty flat, and the prayer mat.

'I'm cold. The dirt must have been keeping me warm.'

She laughed at the joke but his teeth began to chatter in earnest. He rushed to fling himself down on the rug, for the high sofa was his father's bed, and pulled the blanket over him, and sneezed several times. If there had been a stove or wood, she would have lit it, but as she searched anxiously for something to protect him from the cold and allay her fears for him, she found nothing there except herself. Making him turn his back towards her, she took him in her arms, thrusting forward her legs and stomach to encompass him, holding him tight until gradually he stopped trembling.

A great feeling of tranquillity crept over him, while she was intoxicated, her work done, like a mother who has given suck. But she recognized that her emotion was not because she had warmed him and he had grown still and passive, momentarily savouring a mother's embrace: for him it was a stage on the way to other quite different feelings – not of physical desire, but of something stronger, of tenderness and affection – and she might have been expected to respond to the change, to the strangeness in him, and not to the familiar and accessible. But from utter terror she stifled all such feelings within her.

The second square

Call it love or something else, she did not doubt the depth of her feelings: no one on the face of the earth was dearer to her, even her own children. He meanwhile had found a refuge unlike anything he had known; his drug-addicted father, the women who lusted after him and pressed against him on the narrow stairs, all the miseries in his life, faded into oblivion, and in his rebirth all his dreams were incorporated and past and future deprivations made good.

Call it love, or heaven – and the supreme happiness to him just then might well have been to abandon himself to the dreams which began to dislodge him from reality and bear him gently to sleep; just as her dozing could have been a sign of satisfaction after years of gnawing hunger.

But far away from them and their minds' visions of delight, their bodies were in contact, without an intermediary, leaving their minds to drift where they would while they formed irreversible links.

Bodies don't imagine and dream; they only know how to express themselves by clinging together and holding each other in love or hate, while dreams have imagined confrontations in an intangible world. The physical attraction began against the wills of both of them.

He curled up and grew smaller, in imperceptible movements, as

if, left to himself, he would have buried his way into her like a
foetus. She, with the decisive behaviour of one who has made up
her mind to be in opposition, sought to reunite him with his
strangely curled-up physical existence, and with his life – his
father, the room, his clothes hanging up to dry. She began with his
hand – which she had saved, with foresight, from an untoward
action – squeezing it in her own fingers, but then took all of him to
her as if to put him back where he belonged. The feeling of love
which has no physical element at the outset, formed in the
imagination, is changed vehemently by close proximity, although
the imagination, the idea of the love, and the sensibilities, still par-
ticipate in the physical attraction which flares up. And even if he
had been an angel and she a saint, or if the punishment for it was
burning alive, or death at the stake, if the whole world had joined
forces to stop them, the outcome would have been the same. The
strength of such attraction is part of the mystery and power of life,
and suggests that there is a stronger commitment in the scheme of
things to uniting what is separate, than to mere propagation and
survival.

When mutual affection creates attraction, and then the two
beings touch, nothing can come between them. She called upon the
saints and the holy men of God, and the Sayyida; upon her past
self-control, her father's fond smile, her late mother with ten
pilgrimages to her name; and she uttered verses of the Qu'ran, and
all the imprecations she knew to drive out devils. And he sought
help in the teachings of his Sufi sect and with his shaykh and in
the other commands and prohibitions heaped up in his memory.
But the hunger of flesh for flesh, the thirst of mouth for mouth, and
the urge of legs to twine themselves around legs always triumphs.

Their two bodies lying close were heirs to laws of life more complicated and awesome than all the struggles of humanity to escape
from them. What lay between them still was the torment of
suppressed emotions that exploded triumphantly from time to
time, and forbidden areas, which became accessible by degrees.
She clung grimly to her last line of defence as a mother whose
children were successful, educated, and in desperation she invoked
them as a protection in the existing situation and a guard against
what was to come – a safeguard at least from the sensations that
were gradually paralyzing her will. Her intention was to stop the

gaping void in her consciousness of herself as a mother, restrain her power to give from reaching its limit, at which point, God forbid, it would take only a simple impulse to turn it into a desire to take, a particularized desire for him as he lay small, egg-like, waiting.

All this time his longing for her as a mother was reaching unbearable proportions, so that he wanted her for himself exclusively, to a degree that would mean she was barred from all other human relationships. The superficial characteristics of motherliness were not enough for him and he searched straining to reach, and capture for himself, the centre and essence of the motherliness in her: the mother can always accommodate herself to any number of children, but only one man gets the woman and she is his alone.

Their reactions to each other, bold sometimes, embarrassed and inhibited at others, took place in the presence of a long history of rules and prohibitions, eclipsed from time to time by other laws of life which asserted themselves more strongly. He would begin to behave like a lover and she would scold him like a mother, or she would hold him hoping to quieten him down and her motherly embrace would catch fire; and the four, the son and the woman, and the mother and the young man, would show no mercy to each other, nor to spectres from their present lives or others made sacrosanct by the passing of time. In the flame of the rising heat things burnt which are considered incombustible, and prohibitions melted away. The past and the future disintegrated, leaving only the woman taking refuge in the mother in her, and the son distraught, seeking the female hidden inside this mother.

But after all, and however much the affair may seem to have become of purely sensual concern directed by automatic responses, the human body possesses a strange and magical member, the mind, without whose participation and concurrence it would not move an inch independently.

She made a desperate effort: she had summoned her children before her like an army of storm-troopers and from their ranks leapt her grandchildren condemning their grandmother's behaviour, while their fathers looked at her through the scornful eyes of their wives. She thought of her husband and the years of struggle after his death, and her dogged refusal to marry again; past history massed to ward off one decisive moment in the present. As if in

answer to her fervent prayers the miracle happened and the
mother and celibate widow resumed control, the horror of what
she was doing struck her forcibly and she let him go.

Perhaps it was because he had little past to be aware of, or else it
was a characteristic of the difference in their ages, but he could not
bring himself back to the present or hide the desire which had
begun to blind him. He had reached the point where it was too late
for him to stop or go back. Just as it was inconceivable that the
situation should have arisen, so it was now inconceivable that it
should be reversed.

The third square

The squares, whose surface was eaten away and whose edges
protruded unevenly, were the big white stone tiles of the floor in the
flat. The worn cheap rug was not enough to camouflage their
rough edges, and they and the high sofa and the three-legged metal
table and the window full of washing spread out to dry were their
witnesses. They were witnesses not to the fact that a woman in her
fifties had gone home with a boy of eighteen – walking although
she'd twisted her ankle – nor to the fluctuations of rejection and
desire; more accurately perhaps to a battle being waged inside
each one of them. The nature of the battle was obscure and ill-
defined because clouds of varying degrees of embarrassment
swirled about it and enveloped the surrounding area: there was to
start with the simple embarrassment of the mother and son
recognizing each other as man and woman, and suddenly the lover
in him came to the fore and he embraced her neck and covered it
with kisses. They were frenzied boyish kisses, and she whispered
firmly:

'You mustn't do that. I'm old enough to be your mother. My
children are older than you. I'm a grandmother, don't you believe
me?'

As speech had ceased to have any effect she used her hand,
pushing him away gently as a mother would to a son who was
annoying her. And the annoying son advanced upon her insistently
once more, so she showed him the grey hairs, to make him believe,
only to discover, with him, that this inflamed him more. Whenever
she portrayed herself in the image of his mother or tried to evoke

filial responses in him, this had an effect the reverse of what she had
intended, on a youth who now appeared to be aroused by the very
fact that she was a mother, his mother. Worse still, every time she
convinced herself that his behaviour so far fell within the definition
of what could be properly expected of a son, she felt impulses
rearing up inside herself which frightened her because they made
her unfamiliar to herself. The characteristics of this woman were
not in keeping with the one who had been a dutiful daughter whom
her parents had brought up, educated and married off so that she
could beget children who bore children in their turn. She was more
feminine than anything she had imagined in her life about herself
as a woman, and she was imprisoned, and rumbling menacingly,
threatening an explosior. whose repercussions would extend God
alone knew how far. These impulses, this unfamiliar woman in her,
were like a powerful extension of her motherhood, reaching out,
and she had an unconquerable wish to engulf him and possess him,
to make him once again a part of her, because, with her children
there looking on, this boy, this stranger, still seemed to her closer
and more son-like than any of them.

And he wavered between shyness of her and desire for her, shy
even of his masculinity, but shyer still of her femininity. It was as if
he wanted to distil the motherly qualities in her until he found the
woman, or to take the motherly feelings in her which were
exclusively for him, and manipulate them until they became those
of a lover. But be she mother or lover, it no longer satisfied him to
clasp her to him or lie still in her embrace. He moved to her
impetuously to join with her, to be absorbed into her and
extinguished, like a planet returning to its mother star after a long
weary circling.

For all that had passed, there was something inside her which
hadn't stopped since the shrine. It reminded her continually of its
presence and shouted at the top of its voice: 'No . . . no . . . no.' It
had grown fainter sometimes, perhaps, but all the while it was
really gathering momentum, until she started up, pushing him
away with all the fierce strength she possessed. As if a sharp object
had hit him on the head, he woke from his reverie, the rejected
orphan, sensing the unreality of what had charmed him.

It was only then that tears began to gather in his eyes in spite of
himself and run down his face, and he looked straight in front of

him, grief-stricken, without hope: his mother was lost to him and he was like a child standing alone, watching other children with their mothers and fathers dancing up and down for joy.

This was the expression bathed in tears that she had noticed when she glanced sideways at him, and that had stopped her in her tracks. Come what may, she could never let him feel bereaved a second time; it was the glance of a mother to a son at a crucial moment which threatened to call her motherhood into question. And these were the impetuous huggings and kissings that washed away his tears and caressed his broken features.

'Why were you pushing me away then?'

'I won't do it again.'

It wasn't an answer, but a decision. And she acknowledged that she might go straight to hell for it.

'Come here. Come to me.'

She didn't take him in her arms nor did he take her. The distance between them that had remained so great all along was swallowed up, and time evaporated.

The lightning flash as the two poles made contact rocked the square-tiled floor and rattled the windows, and would have brought the whole house down if it had gone on for longer.

The fourth square

When she went back to her big flat, she found it small, and in the mirror the expression reflected there was one she hadn't seen for thirty years.

When the next Friday came, her children were all surprised at the old woman that they had intended her to be, bursting with life, more mobile and energetic than them, and exuding joy like a girl again.

'Didn't I tell you – the Sayyida's done wonders already!'

It was quite unprecedented when she was the first to make her excuses, and her pretext was ready-made: the Sayyida couldn't wait.

There were many catastrophes in the universe, many disruptions in the ordering of human affairs, but the regularity of her appointments with the Sayyida was never broken. After she had filled their stomachs with food and nourished them with a strange tenderness, like a spurt of oil from an abandoned well, and cared for them, and smothered them with maternal feelings, which had become almost too much for them to take, she made her excuses and went to visit the Sayyida.

And every time, with terror, she caught sight of the saint's shrine in the distance and muttered 'Forgive me'.

It was as if time had ceased to exist for her and had no effect on her life, since she had met him. The day when it moved on again was one that she had always taken into her calculations, and foreseen coming, but still when it came she was surprised. She stood where she was, confused, not wanting to believe that the hand wasn't there this time and wouldn't lead her to the room of squares in Hanafy.

When the hours went by and he didn't appear, she began making her way hesitantly to the shop, which was not far from the mosque and the Sayyida's shrine. But she came to a halt before she reached it. He was there, the owner of the shop since his father died, but he was not alone. In front of the shop was a girl, about eighteen, perhaps less – and she did not cease to wonder at the perfection with which she had wound her robe about her. He was haggling with her about the repair of a calor gas stove in words that were full of intimacy and hinted at an understanding of another sort, and the girl was laughing and he was smiling.

She looked at him with new eyes, as if she hadn't seen him properly since the first time, the first time . . .

He was quite different, unshaven, and his beard had begun to grow profusely, black and thick. His laughter was manly, less sweet, and his voice was harsher, with a decisive note. He no longer looked at the world with welcoming eyes and marvelled at it, but looked only to mark out his own path in it. He had grown up, that was clear, joined the ranks of men, where mothers are a burden.

She felt no need to give vent to her misery, and she could stop the world spinning round her, for she wasn't annoyed or sad or surprised, nor even resentful towards the girl, or him. She realized in a vague way, with no ill-feeling, that she too no longer had anything to give him, no more motherliness, no more feelings of any sort; the lush green volcano had run dry.

In the mirror of her handbag she examined her grey hairs, quite visible despite the dye, and the lines around her eyes and on her neck. And she moved away, in the direction of the mosque.

Secretly she asked forgiveness, and it was as if it were granted, for in her humility and submission a desire came to her, and she went towards the saint's shrine.

She stood there for a long time, not knowing what to say or do. Then she had an inspiration, or obeyed an instinct, and approached the brass wall surrounding the shrine. Alongside the other men and women there she grasped one of the burnished brass rings worn down with much use. She gripped it tightly, clinging to it as if the ground at her feet was opening to swallow her up.

No one needed her now, and she needed no one. This was real loneliness as she had never imagined it could be. Like the first signs of winter, noiselessly, it had come. There was no escaping from it: it was as decisive as the change which made her son into someone else's father, or her as she had been into her as she was now, returning to be a daughter, to a mother that didn't exist.

Perhaps that was why they called her Mother of the Helpless, for a human being is no longer a human being, if not father or mother, son or daughter. When a man's manhood, and his fatherhood, is at an end, he becomes a son again, and the same is true for a woman – a rule with no exceptions. But just for the moment she was utterly alone, like Sayyida Zaynab herself who was surrounded by men and women clinging to the rings on the outside of her shrine, each one of them alone like her, driven on by the hope that they could become sons and daughters again – their best hope the saint, the mother of those who have nothing.

And the saint was alone in her grave while the crowd jostled around it, desperate to the point of tears to catch hold of one of the rings and extricate themselves from their loneliness, feeling that in her they had found a mother, even if she were mother of them all. She was alone in her grave. And around her the men and women clung alone.

God have mercy on the saint as well as all of them.